"No way."

"Carter. Come on, think about it. Really think about it. What if it doesn't work out? What if...one of us falls in love and the other doesn't?" *What if one of us is already in love?* "What if it ends up destroying our friendship, our partnership, everything? Then what?"

He just wouldn't listen. "That's not going to happen."

"You can't be sure of that."

"Yes, I can. Nobody's falling in love. That's the beauty of it. We know who we are with each other. We're going to have a great life together, Paige, a *happy* life. That falling-in-love crap isn't going to happen to us."

But it's already happened to me.

* * *

THE BRAVOS OF JUSTICE CREEK:
Where bold hearts collide under Western skies

Dear Reader,

It's almost Christmas in Justice Creek, Colorado, and Paige Kettleman has pulled her life together. She's survived the tragic death of her beloved parents and the desertion of the man who was supposed to love her forever. Her younger sister, Dawn, whom Paige raised alone after their parents died, is just about to graduate from high school—with honors. Paige loves her job. Her boss, Carter Bravo, is also her best friend. The future looks bright ahead.

Until four days before Thanksgiving, when a silly magazine quiz changes everything. The quiz poses the question, "Is he really your best friend or are you secretly in love with him?" And by the time all twenty questions have been answered, Paige is very much afraid that her best friend and business partner has somehow laid claim to her cautious heart.

She really doesn't want to love him. After all, she's been burned before and she doesn't want to go there again. If only she can keep him from ever finding out how she really feels.

But then Carter starts having a few new ideas of his own. He's suddenly realizing that pulled-together Paige is just the woman for him. Carter knows what he wants for Christmas, and he's not giving up until he's made Paige his own.

Happy holidays, everyone,

Christine Rimmer

Carter Bravo's Christmas Bride

Christine Rimmer

ISBN-13: 978-0-373-65926-5

Carter Bravo's Christmas Bride

This edition published by arrangement with Harlequin Books S.A.

For questions and comments about the quality of this book, please contact us at CustomerService@Harlequin.com.

Printed in U.S.A.

Christine Rimmer came to her profession the long way around. She tried everything from acting to teaching to telephone sales. Now she's finally found work that suits her perfectly. She insists she never had a problem keeping a job—she was merely gaining "life experience" for her future as a novelist. Christine lives with her family in Oregon. Visit her at christinerimmer.com.

Books by Christine Rimmer

Harlequin Special Edition

The Bravos of Justice Creek

The Good Girl's Second Chance
Not Quite Married

The Bravo Royales

A Bravo Christmas Wedding
The Earl's Pregnant Bride
The Prince's Cinderella Bride
Holiday Royale
How to Marry a Princess
Her Highness and the Bodyguard
The Rancher's Christmas Princess

Bravo Family Ties

A Bravo Homecoming
Marriage, Bravo Style!
Donovan's Child
Expecting the Boss's Baby

Montana Mavericks: What Happened at the Wedding?

The Maverick's Accidental Bride

Montana Mavericks: 20 Years in the Saddle!

Million-Dollar Maverick

Montana Mavericks: Rust Creek Cowboys

Marooned with the Maverick

Montana Mavericks: The Texans are Coming!

The Last Single Maverick

Visit the Author Profile page at Harlequin.com for more titles.

For my dear friend Carol Sue Ell,
who loves books as much as I do
and is always ready with a kind word.
Thanks for the smiles, Carol Sue,
and for making every day just a little bit brighter.

Chapter One

It all started three days before Thanksgiving with a silly magazine quiz.

Paige Kettleman and her best friend and business partner, Carter Bravo, sat in the plush Denver offices of Leery International Drilling. They were waiting to meet with president and CEO Deacon Leery, who had already commissioned five big-ticket custom-redesigned cars from their company, Bravo Custom Cars.

Carter was getting fidgety. He spent most of his working life in old jeans and T-shirts, with his head stuck under the hood of one of his soon-to-be beautiful custom creations. He'd never enjoyed taking meetings.

But Deacon was a major customer. And Deacon liked Carter to come to his gorgeous office and listen to him ramble on about classic cars for a while before getting around to the dream ride he wanted Carter to build for him next. As far as Deacon was concerned, Paige didn't really even need to be there. But she ran the business end of Bravo Custom Cars. She always went along to visit Deacon for that special moment when they started talking money.

Carter had already taken off his sport coat and tossed it across the back of his chair. Now he sat forward, elbows on his spread knees. He braced his square jaw on his big fist and tapped his booted foot impatiently.

Paige watched him and tried not to grin.

He sent her a quick, challenging glance. "So what? I hate sitting around. That's a crime?"

She stifled a chuckle. "Who said a word about crimes?"

He grunted. "Smug. You know you are. Sitting there all cool and calm in your preppy little suit, tap-tap-tapping on your tablet."

She gave him a bland smile. "I'm sure it won't be long now."

He grumbled something. She wisely did not ask him what. And then he grabbed one of the glossy magazines from the low table in front of them. Hitching one boot across the other knee, he slumped back in his chair and began thumbing through it.

She returned her attention to her tablet and her email correspondence with Kelly Cobb, the Realtor they'd hired a few weeks before. Bravo Custom Cars was looking to expand. Electric cars were the future, and Carter wanted to start building custom electric cars along with the gas hogs most of his clients favored.

Carter and Paige had their eye on a new location. They'd made one offer and been turned down. The owner had rocks in his head. Nobody else in town wanted that property. The building and large fenced concrete yard had been sitting on an ugly stretch of Arrowhead Drive on the outskirts of their hometown for over a year with a big For Sale sign on the gate. Paige and Carter were waiting for the seller to get real and lower his asking price a little before they tried again.

Carter nudged her with his elbow. "You got a pen?" She took one from her black leather tote and handed it over. "Thanks. You listening?"

"Um."

"Good. Because you'll love this. 'Is he really your best friend or are you secretly in love with him?' It's a quiz and you need to take it."

She zipped off the email to the Realtor. "No, I don't."

"Yeah, you do. It's all about us."

Paige reached over and snagged the corner of the magazine so she could get a look at the front of it. "*Girl Code*? You're reading *Girl Code*?"

"I'm broadening my horizons, trying to understand women better. Everyone says I need to."

She stifled a snort and pointed at the other magazines on the low table. "There's a *Car and Driver* right there."

His broad shoulders lifted in a dismissive shrug. "I've read that one. First question. 'Do you compare all your dates to him?' You know you do. So that's a yes." He scratched at the page with the pen she'd foolishly given him.

"It's obvious you don't even need me here," she wryly observed.

He actually had the nerve to smirk. "You're right, I don't. I know all the answers. Because, face it, I know you better than *you* know you—which proves I know a thing or two about women, after all."

"So then shut up," she muttered out of the corner of her mouth. "Take the damn thing silently if you just *have* to go there." A text popped up from Mona, who ran their front office. Mona was closing up for the night. Paige sighed and replied Still @ Leery's. C U 2morrow.

And Carter went right on to the next question. "'Can you tell him anything without feeling at all uncomfortable?' Oh, hell to the yes." He scratched on the page again.

"That's not fair. You have no idea the things I *don't* tell you." There weren't a lot of them, to be strictly honest. But he didn't need to know that right now.

"Oh, come on. You tell me *everything*, Paige. That's how you are with me. Constant oversharing. A thought pops in your head and I'm the only one there? Comes right out your mouth." She elbowed him. Hard. He snickered, leaned away from her so she couldn't do it again and asked, "'Do you care about his happiness more than you do the happiness of your other friends?'" Another snicker as he checked the answer. "'Do you think about drunk-texting him every other weekend?' I'm going with yes for that, too, because if you were drunk, you *know* it would be me you drunk-texted."

Best to just ignore him, she decided. So she did—or at least she pretended to.

And he kept right on, asking the questions and answering them for her. There were twenty in all.

When he finally answered the last one, he announced, "You scored twenty out of twenty. Hate to break it to you, Paige. But you're desperately in love with me."

She considered taking off one of her high-heeled shoes and bopping him on the head with it. But if she hit him once, she would only want to hit him again.

He tossed the magazine back on the table. "I gotta ask."

"No, you don't."

"Why does every woman I meet just *have* to fall in love with me?" he went on as though she hadn't spoken. "I don't get it."

She scoffed, "You're not the only one."

"Wait a minute, hold on. We both know *you* get it. We just found out you're hopelessly in love with me like all the rest of them, remember? So, what is it that you adore about me?"

"Not a thing."

"I think we need to make a list."

"Carter, stop."

He was wearing that smile now. The one that drove all the women right out of their panties—except for her. As his best friend, Paige reminded herself, she was totally immune to that smile. And he was still talking. "Yes. Definitely. Let's make a list."

"Let's not and say we did."

He started ticking off his supposed lady-killing qualities. "Okay, I'll admit it. I'm better looking than most. And I have a great personality. I'm a god in bed—not that you would know that. And I'm well off, but come on. Half the time, I'm covered in axle grease." He gave her one of those looks, serious and teasing, both at the same time. "Paige."

"What?"

"We both know I'm not really all that."

"You think I'm going to argue with you and tell you you're wonderful and not to run yourself down? Ha. Think again."

He spread his arms wide and she had to jerk back in

her chair to keep from getting smacked in the chest with a rock-hard forearm. "Why can't someone explain it to me? What is this thing I have?"

Before Paige could manufacture a suitably quelling reply, the receptionist said pleasantly, "Mr. Leery will see you now."

So they got up and entered the inner sanctum where another plum project was waiting for them.

An hour later, they shook hands with Deacon Leery and wished him a happy Thanksgiving. It had gone well. Carter was excited about acquiring and redesigning his next four-wheeled masterpiece. Paige felt pleased with the deal she'd struck. A satisfying transaction in every way.

Except for that damn quiz. For some reason, she couldn't stop thinking about it.

Ridiculous. Why even worry about it? It was nothing but fluff. Silly, meaningless fluff.

"You're quiet," Carter said about midway through the hour-and-a-half drive back to their hometown of Justice Creek.

She made a sleepy noise, closed her eyes and leaned against the passenger-side window, hoping he'd assume she must be napping and leave her alone.

It worked. But Paige was not napping. Far from it. Her brain was packed to bursting with that absurd *Girl Code* quiz.

Let it go, she told herself. *It's no big deal. Forget about it.*

But she couldn't forget. It was stuck in her mind and it wouldn't go away. It was like the avalanche that killed her parents, a snowball rolling downhill, quickly gaining speed and mass until it buried everyone and everything in its path.

They weren't even her answers, she reminded herself. They were Carter's.

But unfortunately, his answers were the ones that she would have given. And for a silly, meaningless magazine quiz, well, they were kind of good questions, she had to admit.

They were *telling* questions.

And that was why she couldn't put it out of her mind. Carter *had* answered the questions just as she would have. And that meant she couldn't stop thinking that it might actually be true, that she'd gone and fallen secretly in love with her best friend.

And now just look at her, with that totally unacceptable secret loose and wreaking havoc in her mind and heart.

The only good news?

Nobody else knew. Not even Carter. He had no clue. She was dead certain of that. Thank God. He'd only been messing with her, taking that ridiculous quiz for her. He had no idea what he'd done.

The next morning, when he stopped by the house to walk the dogs and then fix breakfast for her and him and her younger sister, Dawn, he seemed totally oblivious. And then at work that day, he mostly stayed in the shop and she managed to stick to the office, so he had no chance to notice if she acted strange and preoccupied.

Mona, who worked side by side with her, caught on, though. "You okay, Paige? You seem kind of far away."

"Christmas on my mind, I guess," Paige outright lied. "And you know, it's kind of quiet today. We should get out the decorations, get them up. You think?"

Mona loved Christmas. She zipped right out to the shed by the back gate and hauled the boxes of decorations up front to the office. They spent a couple of hours setting up the fake tree and tacking sparkly garland on every available surface. Mona already had her old iPod loaded up with Christmas favorites. She stuck it in the dock at the end of the service counter. Holiday tunes filled the air. Mona hummed along under her breath, thrilled to have the office full of Christmas and no longer worrying about what might be bugging Paige.

Wednesday morning when Paige followed the tempting smells of frying bacon and perfectly brewed coffee downstairs, she found the dogs—her beagle, Biscuit, and Carter's hound, Sally—sprawled contentedly on the kitchen floor after their morning walk.

Carter stood at the stove. He had his back to her. She hesitated in the doorway in her flannel pj's and plaid robe and watched him cooking up the bacon nice and slow.

He liked to come over before she and Dawn got up, especially lately, since he'd broken up with his last girlfriend, Sherry Leland. Lately, Carter ended up at Paige and Dawn's a lot of the time. He would take Biscuit out with Sally, then let himself back in and start breakfast.

And even when he had a girlfriend, Carter still found time to walk Paige's dog and brew her morning coffee two or three days a week. Most Sunday nights, he came over for dinner and stayed on to play video games or stream a movie.

That he spent so much time at the Kettlemans' always bugged his girlfriends eventually. They didn't really like that his best friend was a woman and his business partner. They also didn't like that his best friend's teenage sister was kind of a cross between a daughter and a little sister to him. Paige got why it bugged them. She wouldn't like it, either, if her special guy spent most of his working life and half his free time with another woman. Paige used to suggest to him that maybe he should focus more on the girlfriend of the hour and not so much on hanging with her and Dawn.

He wouldn't listen. He said he liked being with her and Dawn, and if his girlfriend was jealous, she needed to get over that.

Paige always felt kind of sorry for Carter's girlfriends. Somehow they all fell so hard for him. And the deeper they fell, the more he pulled away from them. And the more he pulled away, the more upset they got. There would be scenes. Carter hated scenes, mostly because his childhood had been one long, dramatic scene.

His mother, Willow Mooney, had loved his father, Franklin Bravo, to distraction. Franklin was already married when he met Willow. But Frank Bravo didn't let a little thing like a wife get in his way. He set Willow up in a house on the south side of town. Willow kicked Frank out of that house on a regular basis. But she always took him back, remaining his mistress for over two decades, giving Frank five children while he was still married to his first wife, Sondra, who gave him four.

Yeah. Falling for Carter? Not a wise move.

This can't really be happening, Paige thought for about the fiftieth time since Monday and that awful, terrible, silly, pointless quiz. *This can't be happening to me.*

But if it wasn't, then why was she lurking in the doorway to the kitchen, staring longingly at Carter's broad, thick shoulders and fine, tight butt?

It just made her feel sad. Beyond sad. Carter's shoulders and butt had never mattered in the least to her before Monday. Why should they mean so much now?

He sent her a quick smile over one of those far-too-fine shoulders of his. "Coffee's ready."

As if she didn't know. Carter was a great cook. And he had a way with coffee. She would know a Carter-brewed cup of coffee blindfolded. All it took was one sniff. Heaven in a cup.

"Thanks." She shuffled over and filled a mug with the hot, wonderful brew. And then she stood there, leaning against the counter, sipping it slowly, her heart breaking at the hopeless absurdity of it all as Carter cracked eggs into her mother's favorite cast-iron pan.

Carter woke on Thanksgiving morning to the sound of his cell ringing. He stuck out a hand, snared the damn thing off the nightstand and squinted at the display. It was 5:49 and his mother was calling.

When had Willow Mooney Bravo ever climbed out of bed before six in the morning? Never, that he could remember. Even when he and his brothers and sisters were small they knew not to bother Ma too early in the morning. She tended to throw things if you messed with her beauty sleep.

His sweet redbone coonhound, Sally, lifted her floppy-eared head from the foot of the bed and blinked at him questioningly.

"Hell if I know," he said to the dog, and put the phone to his ear. "Ma? What's going on? Did somebody die?"

"Happy Thanksgiving, darling. Everything is fine and no one has died. But I know you're an early riser and I wanted to catch you before you left the house. I want a private word with you—today, I hope. I'm leaving for Palm Springs tomorrow and I'm not sure when I'll be back." Since his father had died four years ago, you could hardly catch his mother at home. She traveled the world, flitting from one luxury destination to the next. "I wonder if you could drop by for a drink before you join the rest of the family at Clara's."

His half sister Clara Bravo Ames had invited the whole family to her house that afternoon for a big Thanksgiving dinner. Paige and Dawn were coming, too. "Won't you be at Clara's?"

"It was sweet of Clara to include me, but no. Big family gatherings exhaust me and I have an early flight tomorrow morning—and besides, I want to speak with you alone."

He didn't really like the sound of that. "About what?"

"Darling. Honestly. Don't be so suspicious. I'll explain everything when we talk."

"We're talking now." At the foot of the bed, Sally picked up the tension in his voice and whined. He snapped his fingers and she slinked up the bed, slithered in a circle and settled beside him where he could throw an arm around her and scratch her silky red head.

His mother went on, sounding way too casual for his peace of mind. "How about this? I know you're expected at Clara's at three. So let's say two o'clock at my house, just you and me." Her house was the Bravo Mansion, which his father had built for his first wife, Sondra. The mansion was full of beautiful things that used to be Sondra's. When Sondra died, Frank married Willow and installed her at the mansion. By then, Carter had been twenty-three and on his own. He'd never had to live in the house he still considered Sondra's, and he was damn

glad he hadn't. He didn't want to go there today, either.
"Carter. Are you still there?"

He patted Sally's smooth flank. "Yeah."

"Two o'clock, then?"

He reminded himself that she was his mother and he really didn't see her all that often these days. "Yeah, Ma. See you then." Disconnecting the call, he tossed the phone on the nightstand. Then he turned to Sally. "Walk?"

Sally let out a happy whine of agreement and lifted off her haunches enough to give a wag of her red tail.

"Let's go pick up Biscuit and get after it, then."

Ten minutes later, he stood on Paige's front porch and stuck his key in the lock. Biscuit was waiting on the other side. He grabbed the beagle's leash from the hook by the door and clipped it to Biscuit's collar. Then he clicked his tongue and Biscuit trotted out the door to wiggle over and butt against Sally, who waited patiently for Carter to lock up again so they could get going.

Half an hour later, he was back in the kitchen at Paige's, getting the coffee going, trying to decide between French toast and oatmeal. He settled on the oatmeal because of the huge dinner ahead of them at Clara's. Paige and Dawn came down together as he was turning off the fire under the oats.

Through breakfast, Dawn chattered away as usual about the afternoon dinner at Clara's, about how she and her best friend, Molly D'Abalo, were going to the movies with friends in the evening.

Dawn was a great kid. Not an ounce of bitterness in her, though she'd lost her mom and dad suddenly when she was only ten. Erica and Jerry Kettleman had been buried in an avalanche while off on a twenty-fifth anniversary skiing trip. Paige had come home from college to take care of her little sister. Together, they'd made it work. And now, at eighteen, Dawn had boundless enthusiasm and a smile for everyone. She was an A student and first chair clarinet with her high school band.

Babbling away happily between bites, Dawn inhaled her oatmeal. Once her bowl was empty, she jumped up, carried it to the sink, ran water in it and rushed off upstairs to get dressed.

Carter turned to Paige, who wore her heavy plaid robe, with her brown hair loose and uncombed on her shoulders. Her eyes looked kind of puffy. She'd hardly said a word since she came downstairs. "You okay?"

She blinked and seemed to shake herself. "Uh. Fine."

"Sure?"

"Positive."

He couldn't really get a read on her, couldn't decide whether he ought to keep pushing her to tell him what was going on with her or let it go. It was odd. As a rule, he never had to push her to tell him if she had a problem. She always came right out with it and asked his advice.

Okay, so maybe this time she needed a little encouragement. He was just about to try that when she jumped up. "Thanks for the breakfast, Carter. You're the best."

"Gotta keep my girls fed." He watched her bustle to the sink, rinse out her bowl and bend to stick it in the dishwasher.

"Well." She shut the dishwasher door and straightened. "Better get after it. The day's not getting any younger. Leave everything. I mean it. I'll clean up."

"Will do."

"Quarter of three?"

"I'll be here."

And then she darted to the door and took off down the hall.

He didn't get it. They always spent a few minutes together in the morning after Dawn went back upstairs. But today—and for the past couple of days, now that he thought about it—Paige couldn't get away fast enough.

Her rush to leave the kitchen right after breakfast hadn't bothered him much yesterday or the day before. Today, though, he'd really wanted to tell her about the weird call from his mother. He wanted to get her take on Willow suddenly asking him to come to the Bravo Mansion and have a drink with her, alone.

But so much for wanting Paige's input.

"So, okay, then," he said to the dogs, because there was no one else there to hear him. He rose. "Come on, Sally. Time to go."

Built less than forty years ago on top of a hill at the west end of Grandview Drive, the Bravo Mansion seemed a product of a much earlier age. Georgian in style, with big white columns flanking the front door, the mansion bore a striking resemblance to the White House. Let it never be said that Frank Bravo didn't dream big.

The housekeeper, Estrella Watson, must have been told to watch for him. Before he was halfway up the front steps, she pulled the wreath-hung door open and gave him a big smile of greeting. "Happy Thanksgiving, Carter." She reached for a hug.

He wrapped his arms around her. "Good to see you." He'd always liked Estrella. She'd been the mansion's housekeeper for years, from before Sondra died and

Carter's mother moved in. Well into her fifties now, Estrella kept the house and grounds in great shape, hiring and supervising maids, gardeners and repairmen. She lived in, cooking for Willow whenever his mother was at home. She seemed to enjoy her job and treated everyone kindly.

A jumble of boxes filled the front hall, most of them opened, bright decorations and shiny ornaments spilling out. "It's a weeklong job, getting the house ready for the holidays," Estrella explained. "And I'm not preparing Thanksgiving dinner this year, so I thought I might as well get a head start."

What for? he couldn't help wondering. Only she and his mother lived there, and his mother was leaving for California. But Willow liked the mansion just so, whether she stuck around to enjoy it or not. And Estrella had a gleam in her eye, as though nothing pleased her more than decking the halls of the big, empty house.

She took his coat. "Your mother's in the library."

He thanked her and went on through the formal living room to the large book-lined room behind it, where a fire crackled in the ornate fireplace and the mantel was already done up in swags of green garland studded with shiny ornaments and twinkling lights.

"Carter." His mother rose from a silk-covered chair. She looked beautiful as always, in snug black slacks and a fitted green cashmere sweater, her chin-length blond hair combed back from the classic oval of her face.

He kissed the smooth, pale cheek she offered. "Ma. How are you?"

She fiddled with the diamond stud in her left ear. "Perfect. Thank you. How about a martini?"

He looked at her patiently. "Got a beer?"

She sighed. "Of course." She had a longneck waiting in an ice bucket on the fancy mirrored drink cart, right next to the Bombay Sapphire and the Vya vermouth. She also had a chilled glass for him.

"Just give me the bottle."

Another sigh. His mother had been born with nothing. Her own mother ran off when she was three weeks old and Willow grew up in a double-wide, just her and her father. Gene Mooney, deceased before Carter was born, had had trouble holding a job and drank too much. It probably wasn't all that surprising that, over the years, Willow had developed a passion for elegance and gracious living. The way Willow saw it, if a man insisted on drinking beer, he should at least use a glass.

Too bad. Carter took the beer, sat in the chair across from hers and watched as she skillfully whipped up her martini—stirred, not shaken.

Willow took her seat again and raised her glass. "To happiness."

Happiness? His mother had never struck him as a person who put a lot of store in happiness. She'd wanted Frank Bravo and the good life he provided for her. And she'd fought tooth and nail to get both.

But hey. She was getting older. Maybe she missed the happiness that had never seemed all that important to her while Carter was growing up.

"Happiness it is." He lifted his bottle in answer to her toast and resisted the urge to come right out and ask her why she'd summoned him here. It wouldn't kill him to try a little friendly conversation. "So, what's happening in Palm Springs?"

"The usual. Shopping. Spa time. And the weather is lovely there now."

"Well. Have a great time."

"I will, darling."

Ho-kay. So much for cordial conversation. He took one more stab at it. "We'll miss you at Clara's."

She smiled her cool smile. "Somehow I doubt that."

Annoyance gnawed at him. His half siblings had made it more than clear that they wanted to forgive and forget. Her decades-long love triangle was seriously old news. "You're wrong. We *will* miss you." He took care to say it gently. "And I think you know that."

She sipped her drink. "I didn't ask you here to talk about dinner at Clara's."

"Well, all right. What's going on?"

Willow lounged back in the chair and crossed her legs. "Notice I made a toast to happiness?"

"Yeah, Ma. I heard you."

"That's because lately I've been thinking a lot about happiness, about what makes a man—or anyone, really—truly happy." She paused. Just to be nice, Carter made an encouraging sound low in his throat. She said, "Take your brother."

"Which one?" He had two full brothers, both younger than he was—Garrett, thirty-three, and Quinn, thirty-one. And then there were also Sondra's sons, Darius and James.

"I'm talking about Quinn," his mother said. A former martial arts star, Quinn had retired from fighting last year and brought his little daughter, Annabelle, home to Justice Creek. Now he owned a gym and fitness center on Marmot Drive. Just recently, he'd gotten together with gorgeous Chloe Winchester, who'd also grown up in town. "Now that Quinn's married Chloe, he's a truly happy man."

Carter wasn't sure he liked where this was going. "Can't argue with that," he answered cautiously.

"I want that for you, too, darling. I want you to find happiness."

Okay, now. He *definitely* didn't like where this was going. "What are you up to, Ma? Just spit it the hell out."

"Love, darling. I want you to take a chance on love."

He really wished he hadn't asked. "Oh, well, sure. I'll get right on that."

"Don't give me sarcasm. You're thirty-four years old. When a man reaches your age and he's never been married, the likelihood that he'll find someone to be happy with is..." Another sigh. God. He hated her damn sighs. "It's not looking good for you. You have to know that."

Carter sat very still in the silk wing chair and reminded himself not to say anything he would later regret. But she pissed him the hell off. She acted as if he didn't want to get married. He *did.* Very much.

But somehow the whole romance thing never worked out for him. And it wasn't as if he hadn't tried. He had. Repeatedly.

There was just something about him, something *wrong* with him. Because he always attracted the drama queens.

Things would begin well. Lots of fireworks in bed, yes, but otherwise the woman would seem like a reasonable person, someone he could talk to, someone easygoing and fun. Early on, his girlfriends reassured him that they wanted what he wanted, a solid partnership and a balanced life. He always explained up front that he expected an exclusive relationship and he planned someday to get married, but if they were after passionate declarations of undying love, they should find a different guy. The woman would say that was no problem; she completely understood.

But every woman he'd ever dated had eventually told him she loved him. He never said it back. And his silence on the subject never worked for them. The downward spiral would start. There would be heated accusations, generally irrational behavior and a messy breakup at the end. He hated all that.

Truthfully, deep down?

Carter thought the whole love thing was pretty damn stupid. The way he saw it, falling in love was a good way to lose your mind.

His mother said, "I know, darling. I understand. I wasn't a good mother."

"Did I say that? I never said that."

"You don't have to say it. It's simply the truth. There were way too many big dramatic scenes. I loved your father to distraction and I wanted him to leave Sondra. Every time I kicked him out, I swore I would never take him back."

"But you always did."

"I loved him." She said it softly, gently. As though it explained everything.

Carter kept his mouth shut. It was stupid to argue about it. To some people, love excused the worst behaviors. All you had to do was call it love and you could get away with anything—steal someone else's husband, make your children's lives an endless series of shouting matches and emotional upheavals.

His mother set her empty martini glass on the small inlaid table by her chair. "I want you to take a chance on love. I may be a bad mother, but I do love you. And a mother knows her children. At heart, you're like Quinn.

A family man. I won't have you ending up alone because of my mistakes."

She wouldn't *have* it? You'd think he was ten, the way she was talking. "Ma, you really need to dial this back. It's not all about you. I'm a grown man and have been for quite a while now. It's on me if I can't make things work with a woman."

"Not entirely. I know very well that my actions when you were growing up have made you afraid of strong emotions."

He looked at her sideways. "Have you gone into therapy or something?"

"No. I've only been thinking—as I've already told you. These days, I have plenty of time for thinking."

"Well, think about something other than me and my supposed need for true love and a wife, why don't you?"

She didn't answer, only sat there in her chair, watching him for about fifteen seconds that only seemed like an hour and a half. He was just about to jump up, wish her a safe trip to California and get out of there when she said, "I asked you here to offer a little something in the way of motivation, a little something in the interest of helping you get past your fears."

He stood and set his empty beer bottle on the drink cart. "You never suffered from a lack of nerve, Ma. I gotta give you that. Look, this…whatever it is you think you're pulling here is more than I'm up for, you know? You really need to mind your own damn business."

His mother didn't seem a bit bothered by his harsh words. She gave a shrug. "I can that see you're ready to go."

"More than ready."

"Just listen to my offer before you leave. Please."

"Offer? You're kidding me. There's an offer?"

She draped an arm over the chair arm and crossed her legs the other way. "Yes, there is. I know that you and Paige have been eyeing a certain property on Arrowhead Drive, with a large cinder-block industrial building on it."

"What the…? How do you know that?"

She waved a hand. "It was all really quite innocent."

"Innocent," he repeated. Not a word he would think of in connection with Willow. "Right."

She fiddled with her earring again. "I drove by there a few weeks ago and saw the two of you standing outside the gate. And then I recalled how, several months ago, you said something about wanting to expand Bravo Custom Cars. I added two and two. Voilà. Four. Tuesday, I paid a visit to the owner. He had a price. And I have paid it."

"You're not serious."

"Oh, but I am. I've bought that property."

"What for? What possible use can you have for a fifteen-thousand-square-foot cinder-block building and a concrete yard rimmed in chain-link fence?"

"None, of course."

He wanted to pick up his empty beer bottle and hurl it at the garland-bedecked fireplace. "I'm going to leave now, Ma. Happy Thanksgiving and have a nice trip to Palm Springs." He turned to go back through the formal living room and out the way he'd come in.

And she said, "The property is yours, free and clear. But only as a wedding present."

Keep going, he thought. *Don't give her the satisfaction of taking her seriously.* But then he just couldn't let it go at that. He halted and turned back to her. "Reassure me, Ma. Tell me you *didn't* just say that if I get married, you'll give me the property."

"But that is exactly what I said."

Unbelievable. "What if you've got this all wrong? What if Paige and I have zero interest in that property?"

"Ah, but I'm not wrong, am I?"

He could strangle her. He'd probably get the death penalty and go to hell for murdering his own mother. But right at that moment, murder seemed like a great idea. "Just curious. Did you have any particular bride in mind for me?"

"Of course not. It has to be someone you choose for yourself."

He made a low, scoffing sound in his throat. "Wow. I get to choose the woman myself."

"I wouldn't have it any other way."

"I gotta say it, Ma."

"Go ahead. Whatever you need to tell me, I'm here and I'm listening."

"The way your mind works?"

"Yes?"

"It's always scared the hell out of me."

"Don't be cruel. Can't you see that I'm doing this for you? It's a nudge, plain and simple, an opportunity for you to start thinking about giving love and happiness a chance. I just want you to entertain the idea of making a good life with the right woman. The property is an incentive, that's all."

He laughed. Because it was funny, right? And then he said, "You have a great holiday, Ma."

She granted him her coolest smile. "Thank you, darling. I will."

He turned on his heel then. This time, he didn't pause

or turn back. He strode fast through the front room and into the giant foyer, where he collected his coat from Estrella and got the hell out of there.

Chapter Two

Not only was Carter's mother a manipulative nutcase; his best friend had checked out on him.

Carter sat between Paige and Dawn at the long, white-clothed table in his half sister Clara's formal dining room and wondered what was the matter with Paige. She'd hardly said two words to him all afternoon. At some point between the time she'd left the breakfast table that morning and two forty-five in the afternoon, when he picked her and Dawn up to bring them to Clara's, Paige had gotten dressed, combed her hair and put on makeup. But her eyes still had that strange vacant look.

If someone spoke to her directly, she would lurch to life and pretend to be interested. But as soon as the focus moved elsewhere, she'd settle back into the weird funk she'd been in for days now.

Twice, he leaned close and asked her if she was okay.

Both times, she lied. “Fine,” she said the first time. “Great,” she answered later.

He left her alone after that. They could talk about it when they got back to her place.

For now, he enjoyed his family. The food was always good at Clara’s house. Plus, Clara was a truly sweet woman and happily married to a banker from Denver named Dalton Ames. They had a six-month-old daughter, Kiera.

Carter liked hanging around Dalton and Clara. Just seeing them together made him smile. They’d had some difficulties when they first started out, but they’d worked through them and come out strong on the other side.

Same thing with his brother Quinn and Chloe Winchester, who was now Chloe Bravo. Truthfully, Willow might be full of crap about a lot of stuff, but she was right about Quinn and Chloe. Quinn and Chloe had that thing—whatever it was. They shared that special connection, same as Dalton and Clara.

And then there was his cousin Rory and her fiancé, Walker McKellan. Rory Bravo-Calabretti was an honest-to-God princess from the tiny Mediterranean principality of Montedoro. She’d moved to Justice Creek last winter. She and Walker, who owned a guest ranch not far from town, were getting married on Christmas Eve.

And yeah, Rory and Walker had it, too. Same as Clara and Dalton. Same as Quinn and Chloe.

Hanging around at Clara’s house on Thanksgiving, watching those three couples interact with each other, Carter could almost start to think that love and forever were actually possible.

At least for other people.

Once the meal was through, they all helped to clear

the table. Then a little later, Dalton turned the game on in the great room. Some of them—Carter included—gathered around the big screen mounted over the mantel.

Most of the women headed for the kitchen area, which shared the high-ceilinged great room space. Carter could hear them back there, bustling around, laughing and talking over each other, having a fine time. He heard Paige's distinctive husky laugh. Apparently, whatever was bothering her didn't stop her from having fun with his sisters.

Dawn came and sat on the sofa arm next to him. He glanced up at her and she sent him a quick smile. Then Quinn's daughter, Annabelle, who'd recently turned five, wandered over. She was the cutest kid, with a plump little pixie face. Chloe must have done her hair. It was curled and held back with big sparkly barrettes. She wore one of those puffy, lacy dresses that little girls liked to wear, complete with white tights and shiny black Mary Janes. She whispered something to Dawn.

Dawn said, "Absolutely," and swung the little girl up on her knee.

Annabelle leaned back in Dawn's arms as if she belonged there. She caught Carter watching her and said, "I *like* Dawn, Uncle Carter. She's very pretty."

"Yes, she is," he agreed.

Dawn, who'd always been good with kids, cuddled Annabelle closer.

Carter felt a little better about everything, with the two happy girls sitting next to him. He liked his family—his mother excluded, at least at the moment. He liked that Dawn felt comfortable here at Clara's with his siblings and half siblings.

Now, if only he could get Paige to get real about whatever was bugging her. Once they had that out of the way, he could tell her all about the stunt Willow had just pulled and break the bad news that they needed to find another property for the expansion.

After the pie and coffee, Carter drove Paige and Dawn home in the '61 Lincoln he'd taken out of the shop for the day. He was looking forward to being alone with Paige so they could talk.

"Gotta hurry." Dawn was out of the car the second he pulled up to the curb in front of their house. "I'm meeting Molly at the Gold Rush in twenty minutes." The Gold Rush was the movie theater on Golden Drive. She leaned in the rear door she'd just jumped out of. "Thanks, Carter. It was fun."

Paige said, "Home by—"

"Midnight, promise," Dawn finished for her and pushed the door shut.

Carter started to turn off the engine, but Paige said, "I'm really tired. And me and my Visa card have a shopping date tomorrow." Bravo Custom Cars would be closed. It was a BCC tradition to give everyone both Thanksgiving and Black Friday off. Paige went on. "Nell and Chloe and Jody are picking me up at three a.m." Nell and Jody were his sisters. "We're driving into Denver to check out the deals. I need sleep to get ready for a day of serious shopping, so I think I'll draw a hot bath and call it an early night."

He turned off the engine and shifted in the seat to face her. "You mean you don't want me to come in."

She cleared her throat. "Well, as I said. I'm tired and it's going to be a long—"

"Stop it. Tell me what is going on."

"What are you talking about? There's nothing—"

"Paige, you've been dragging around like the world's coming to an end for two or three days now, all the time constantly telling me there's nothing wrong. What's up?"

"Nothing. Really."

"Come on. It's something."

"Nope. Uh-uh. Nothing. Like I said, I'm just really tired."

He gave in. "Fine. Great. Later, then." It was only a ploy. He honestly expected her to hesitate, to say she was sorry for brushing him off, to ask him not to be annoyed with her—something. Anything.

But she only chirped out a quick "Night, then. And thanks. I had a great time," and leaped out of the car.

He watched her run up the front walk and disappear into the house. He just didn't get it. Paige told him everything. In detail. Way too much detail, as a rule.

What could be bothering her that she couldn't talk about it with him?

The next morning, Carter decided he would walk Sally alone. He was kind of pissed at Paige for shutting him out. Why in hell would he want to walk her damn dog for her?

And she was in Denver anyway, right? She wouldn't be there to eat any breakfast he cooked for her.

But then what about Dawn? Paige hadn't mentioned whether Dawn was going, too. What if Dawn was home alone? She'd need breakfast.

And what about poor Biscuit? Biscuit liked his morning walk with Sally.

So Carter and Sally went over to the Kettlemans', after all. He got Biscuit and walked the two dogs. On the way back, he called Dawn on her cell.

She answered with a big yawn. "Yeah, what?"

"You still in bed?"

"How'd you guess?"

He grunted. "Just checking to see if maybe you went to Denver with Paige."

"Uh-uh. Too early for me. You coming to make breakfast?"

"I'm on my way."

He made French toast and tried to be subtle when he asked Dawn if she'd noticed anything different about Paige in the last few days.

Dawn groaned. "Oh, yeah. Something's on her mind. But every time I ask, she tells me there's nothing."

He felt instantly vindicated. And then he frowned. "So…you don't know what it is, either, huh?"

"I'm clueless. Seriously. But how awful can it be, really? I mean, she got up at two-thirty in the morning to spend the day shopping. I don't think it's an incurable disease or anything."

"A disease?" That kind of freaked him out. "It didn't even occur to me she might have a disease…"

"Carter. Pull yourself together."

"Well, I'm worried about her, okay?"

"She's just feeling down about something."

"It's not like her," he grumbled.

"Everybody feels low now and then. Eventually, she'll tell you. She always does."

"Yeah," he said, feeling marginally better. "Of course she will. She always does." He knew everything about Paige, all the little things—that she thought she looked bad in purple and she liked '70s rock.

He knew that she'd been in love with a loser named Jim Kellogg when she was in college. She and Jim had been talking marriage, but he dumped her when her parents died. He said he didn't want to follow her to some Podunk small town and help her raise her sister. Since then, she'd only dated casually.

He asked Dawn, "What time did she say she'd be back from Denver?"

"Five or six—and, Carter?"

"Yeah?"

"Let it go. She'll tell you when she's ready to tell you."

"You're right. I will…"

After breakfast, he took Sally home and then headed for Bravo Custom Cars, thinking about Paige the whole way. About him and Paige, about how they'd hit it off from the start.

He'd met her at Romano's Restaurant, where she'd started working after her parents died. He'd liked her right off and he used to eat there at least a couple of times a week, partly because Romano's had the best Italian food around. But mostly because he loved to sit in Paige's section and give her a hard time. He'd asked her out more than once. She'd turned him down over and over, but he kept trying.

Finally, she'd told him gently and regretfully that she was never going out with him.

She hadn't told him why she wouldn't date him. Not then. The truth had come out later, as their friendship grew. About how she was happier on her own, that her heart had been stomped on but good by that Kellogg creep when she was already in bad shape from losing her parents.

But that was later.

He could still remember her way back at the beginning of their friendship, still see her so clearly, standing by his favorite booth at Romano's, her hands in the pockets of her waitress apron. "I don't need a date, Carter. But I could sure use a friend."

"Then you got one," he'd said.

The overhead fluorescents had brought out red lights in her dark brown hair, and her soft mouth kicked up at the corners. "Does my friend need another beer?"

When he opened BCC, she'd answered his ad for an office manager. He hired her on the spot and she got right after it, moving the furniture around in the office for better "work flow," as she called it, setting up the front counter and the customer waiting area so she could see everything from her desk. He knew cars. Paige knew a whole lot about systems and how to set up the front of the shop. Not only did she seem to have a knack for running the place; she'd been a semester away from getting a BA in business when her parents died and she quit to come home.

The woman knew her way around a spreadsheet. He'd figured out within the first few weeks that he needed to keep her around. So every year at Christmas, he gave her a percentage of the company as her Christmas bonus. Five years after they opened BCC, they were best friends and she owned 25 percent of the business.

They had a good thing going. And somehow, now that she'd cut herself off from him, suddenly everything in his life seemed all wrong. Best friends were supposed to communicate. Paige knew that. Or at least, she always lectured him about communication whenever he got feeling down and wouldn't say what was bugging him.

He unlocked the gate at BCC and sailed onto the lot. Stopping the Lincoln in front of one of the bay doors, he climbed out and went around to the shop's side door, where he turned off the alarm and let himself in. A button by the bay sent the accordion door rumbling up. He pulled the Lincoln into the open bay, got out again and shut the bay door. It was sunny out, but only in the midthirties, so he turned on the heat.

The Lincoln, which he'd customized in a number of pretty cool ways, needed a little fine-tuning. *He* needed to let all this worrying about Paige go. She would talk when she was ready to talk. And when she did, he'd be there to listen.

In the meantime, BCC was closed for Black Friday and he had the whole place to himself. He could get the Lincoln purring like a kitten and ready for the day trader from Boulder who'd commissioned it from him. And then he might even get started on the already cherry '68 Shelby Cobra GT-500 Fastback that Deacon wanted pimped out with a whole new sound system and all the modern conveniences, including GPS. Deacon also wanted a rear spoiler, a modified grille and monster wheels with some really garish rims. It kind of seemed a shame to do that to a work of art like the Cobra. But Deacon didn't pay him the big bucks to suddenly get squeamish over messing with the classics.

Carter had a killer sound system in his shop. He turned on the radio to a hard rock station. As ZZ Top roared out, he zipped up his overalls and got down to it.

He didn't notice he had company until about an hour later, when he rolled out from under the Lincoln and headed for the inner door to the office and the little table in front of the window, where Paige kept one of those K-Cup machines. He had a nice hot mug of coconut mocha on his mind and had all but forgotten that he'd failed to relock the side door to the shop when he came in.

Whipping a rag from his rear pocket, he wiped the worst of the grease from hands and switched off the radio. He loved vintage Bruce as much as the next man, but sometimes a little silence was good for the soul.

As he turned for the front-office door, he registered movement out of the corner of his eye.

And then he saw her: Sherry Leland, his ex-girlfriend.

Sherry had taken the cover off the metal-flake candy-apple-red '67 Firebird just back from the painter's on Wednesday, and draped that killer body of hers across the hood.

"Hello, Carter." She gave him one of her come-and-get-me smiles. The smile matched her outfit: a red thong, a Santa hat and sky-high stilettos.

It was a testament to how over Sherry he really was that his first thought had very little to do with her being nearly naked. His first thought concerned how those pointy heels of hers had to be screwing up the Firebird's high-dollar paint job.

"Sherry," he said and tried not to sigh.

"I thought you'd never come out from under that car." She stuck out her plump lower lip in a sexy pout and tossed her long blond hair. "I'm starting to get kind of chilly." She fluttered her eyelashes and glanced down at her bare breasts. Yep. She was chilly, all right. "Come on over here, baby," she cooed. "Come here and warm me up."

"Sherry, I..." He really wanted to ask her to please get off the hood and be careful while she was doing it. But showing concern for the paint job right at that moment would only send her through the roof.

Her pout started to get kind of pinched looking. "What is the matter with you? I *missed* you. I'm here in this smelly garage of yours practically naked and it's all for you." The big blue eyes suddenly brimmed with fat tears. "I'm here to get past this little problem we've been having. I'm here to prove to you how much I want to work things out."

There was nothing to work out. They were done and she knew it, *had* been done for months now.

He spotted her black trench coat. She'd tossed it on top of the cover she'd whipped off the Firebird. So he stuck his rag back in his pocket, crossed to the coat, grabbed it and held it up for her. "Sherry, come on."

She sniffled. "How can you be so cold? You're breaking my heart. How can you do this to me?"

"Put your coat on," he coaxed.

"Fine. Sure." Sharp heels digging in, she scrambled off the hood. He tried really hard not to wince at the sight. She tossed her hair some more. And then she came at him, hands raised in frustration. "I hate you, Carter Bravo!"

"Sherry, there's no point in—"

"Hate you!" And she hauled back and bitch-slapped him right across the face. That shocked him. She'd never physically attacked him before.

Then all the fight went out of her. She crumpled, burying her head in her hands. The sobs started.

He gently wrapped the coat around her. "It's over," he said quietly. "You know it is."

She sobbed harder. "But I *love* you…"

He took her to the counter at the window between the shop and the office and whipped a few tissues from the box there. "Come on, now. Blow your nose."

She snatched the tissues and swiped at her cheeks.

He said sincerely, "I'm sorry, Sherry. For everything. Let me drive you home."

"Forget it." With a furious sniff, she shoved her arms in the trench he'd draped on her shoulders and tied the belt, hard. Then she raked her acres of hair off her face and aimed her chin high. "I'm not going anywhere with you."

He had no idea what to say next, so he said nothing. She wheeled on one of those pointy heels and stalked toward the side door, flinging it wide when she got there. That door was made of steel. It banged good and loud against the wall. "That does it, Carter. I am through. Finished. I hope I never see your face again."

He kept his mouth shut. He had a feeling that even the sound of his voice right then could have her storming at him all over again. Uh-uh. Better to keep quiet and stand still.

At his extended silence, she fisted both hands at her sides, threw her head back and let out a yowl of frustration. A second later, she disappeared from sight.

Carter stayed right where he was, hardly daring to breathe, until he heard the Camaro he'd rebuilt for her start up. She gunned it and then roared from the lot. He gritted his teeth, hoping against hope that she wouldn't run into anything, wouldn't hurt herself or anyone else.

As the sound of the engine faded into the distance, he let himself breathe again. And then, reluctantly, he took a good look at the Firebird.

Yep. Dents and gouges all over that hood. Resigned, he whipped the cover back in place. Monday, he'd get it back to the paint booth and tell the customer he'd need a few more days before the car would be ready.

It would be okay. Sherry would get over him and eventually move on.

He just wished he knew what was wrong with him. He just wished he could someday find a sane woman to get involved with. His mother had it right about one thing. He'd always known that someday he wanted a family.

Well, the years were going by. And someday was starting to look a whole lot like never. But what the hell was a guy supposed to do? He'd tried over and over and it always ended up the way it had with Sherry. This time, he had zero desire to find someone else and try again.

Chapter Three

Paige had a great day shopping in Denver with Carter's sisters and sister-in-law. She found a bunch of fabulous deals, giving her a serious head start on her Christmas list. The stores were all decked out for the holidays, and Christmas music filled the air, so the day really kind of put her in the holiday spirit. It was good to get out of town and it helped her achieve a little much-needed perspective.

She realized she needed to stop avoiding Carter. It wasn't his fault if she'd suddenly started thinking she might be in love with him—*might* being the operative word.

It was a magazine quiz, for God's sake. What fool took a magazine quiz seriously?

The next morning, there he was as usual when she came downstairs. Her heart leaped at the sight of his handsome face and sexy smile. She thought of how good he was to her and her sister, showing up to walk the dog and fix the breakfast even when she'd been avoiding him for days. That made her misty-eyed.

But Paige didn't let a leaping heart or misty eyes keep her from trying harder that morning. She made an effort to join the conversation, remembering to thank him, to praise his cooking and his coffee. More than once, she caught him glancing her way, questions in his eyes.

She waited until Dawn went back upstairs to call Molly and make plans for their Saturday, before she said, "I'm sorry I've been moody the last few days. Hormones. They drive me crazy sometimes." Yeah, it was a stretch. But not a total lie. She *had* been on her period.

"But you're okay now?" He looked so hopeful.

She promised him that she was. He poured himself more coffee, sat down beside her—and his cell rang. It was Mona, already at the shop, with some unexpected issue that needed his okay.

He said he'd be right over and hung up. "Gotta go. You coming in today?"

"I wasn't planning to." Paige had Saturdays off. Mona took Mondays and they were closed Sundays.

He was already reaching for his jacket. "Talk later? We've got lots to catch up on."

Paige answered him vaguely, "Yeah. Later. Sounds good." Did that mean he'd be over that evening? Was she ready for that? And speaking of talking, she needed to talk to someone about all this, get her head on straight when it came to Carter—and keep it that way.

He clicked his tongue for Sally. "Come on, girl. Time to go." Leveling those clear green eyes on her, he said softly, "Glad you're okay."

"Thanks." She gave him her brightest smile.

Sally at his heels, he left through the back door. Biscuit watched them go from his favorite throw rug at the end of the snack bar, dropping his head to his paws when they were out of sight.

With a grim little sigh, Paige got up and started clearing the table. She was busy wiping counters when Dawn reappeared, fully dressed this time in jeans and a thick blue sweater patterned with a band of snowflakes across the front.

"Molly's coming over in half an hour. We're going to practice together for the Christmas concert." They were both in the school band and in the orchestra, Paige on B-flat clarinet, Molly on flute.

Paige tossed the sponge in the sink—and made a decision. Dawn might be only eighteen, but she had a level head on her shoulders. Paige trusted her absolutely. Who better to confide in than her own sister?

Half an hour should be plenty of time.

Dawn was frowning. "You okay?"

Paige went ahead and answered honestly, "No, not really."

Dawn leaned her head against the doorframe. "You've been acting strangely for days now."

Paige marched to the table and pulled out a chair. "Got a few minutes?"

Dawn joined her, taking the chair next to hers. "Want me to call Molly, tell her to come later?"

"Nah. Half an hour should do it…" Where to even begin?

Dawn braced her chin on her hand. "I'm here. I'm listening."

Paige waded in. "So, last Monday Carter and I went to Denver to meet with one of our biggest customers.

We had to wait awhile to see him and Carter decided I needed to take this stupid quiz..."

Dawn made a sound in her throat, a little grunt of encouragement.

It was all Paige needed. She let the story pour out, about the silly quiz and how Carter answered all the questions for her and then announced that the quiz proved she was hopelessly in love with him. "I know it's ridiculous. He was just giving me a hard time the way he loves to do. But all his answers? They were the answers *I* would have given. And since then, I can't stop thinking about it. Can't stop thinking that the stupid quiz was right, that I'm actually in love with him, with Carter of all people. It's driving me crazy, Dawn."

Dawn reached over and gently squeezed her arm. "I can see that."

"So I want you to tell me the truth now. I want you to tell me that of course I'm not in love with Carter, that I've just gotten hung up on some meaningless magazine quiz and I need to let it go and move on."

Dawn made a pained sound and looked away.

Hesitantly, Paige reached out and ran her hand down Dawn's straight golden-brown hair. It was the same color and texture as their mother's hair had been. Dawn also had their mother's warm hazel eyes. "Dawn?"

Dawn looked at her then—and winced. "Really? I mean, seriously?"

Paige tried a laugh. It came out more like a sob. "Ridiculous, right?"

Dawn clapped both hands to her head, as though she was worried her brains might escape. "Ugh." And then she dropped her hands to the table, slapping her palms flat. "Dude." She rubbed the tender skin beneath her eyes. "I'm just not gonna lie to you. I think you need to get real, you know? I think it's better if the two of you just face the truth."

Paige's stomach lurched and sweat bloomed on her upper lip. "Um, what truth?"

"You've always been in love with him."

Paige gasped. "What the…? No. Uh-uh. Just no."

"Oh, come on, Paige. He practically lives here. You work together and you're best friends and he'd rather be with you than any of those smokin'-hot girlfriends he's had. Paige, come on. Everybody knows—everybody but you and Carter."

Paige slumped in her chair. "I don't believe it. You think I'm in love with him."

"I don't just *think* it, I know it. And he's in love with you."

That had Paige scoffing. "Oh, please. Carter doesn't do love."

"Carter doesn't *admit* love. It's two different things."

Paige let her head drop back and groaned at the ceiling, because honestly, how could this be happening to her?

"You actually wanted me to lie about it straight out." Dawn sounded hurt.

Paige sucked in a fortifying breath and faced her sister. "I'm sorry. Come here." She reached for Dawn, who resisted at first, but then swayed in her chair and finally let herself lean on Paige. Paige stroked her hair. "You're incredible."

"Yeah, right."

Tenderly, Paige admitted, "Okay, I confess. Sometimes it's a little scary to have such a brilliant and perceptive baby sister."

"I wouldn't have said anything," Dawn muttered. "I never have. But you asked me straight out."

Paige rocked Dawn a little, the way she used to do so often during that first terrible year after they lost Mom and Dad. "Please don't be insulted, but I need to ask you not to tell him."

"Of course I won't tell him," Dawn grumbled. "Have I said a word up till now?"

"No, you haven't. You're an angel."

"Hardly." She pushed free of Paige's embrace and said, "*You* need to tell him."

Paige only blew out a hard breath and slowly shook her head.

At 2:10 that afternoon, Carter was in his office off the shop studying engine schematics for Deacon's Cobra.

Someone tapped on the door.

"It's open." Carter glanced up from his laptop as the door swung wide.

Murray Preble, one of Carter's top auto parts vendors, stuck his head in. "Got a minute?"

"Sit." Carter gestured at the empty chair across the desk. Murray closed the door before folding his long, thin frame into the offered seat. Carter frowned. Murray never shut the door when he stopped in to say hi. "Is this a secret meeting, Murray?"

Murray, who was usually a pretty cheerful guy, didn't even crack a smile. "I guess you could say that. I need this to be just between you and me."

Carter shut his laptop. "Is there a problem?"

Murray scraped his hand down his narrow face and smoothed his thick black hair off his forehead. "Well, Carter, it's about Sherry."

Sherry? Murray wanted to talk about Sherry—with the door closed? Cautiously, he asked, "What about her?"

Murray shifted in the chair. And then he straightened up and put it right out there. "I'm in love with her."

This was news. And maybe good news. If Murray and Sherry got together, she would leave Carter alone. "Well, great. I hope you'll be very happy."

"See, that's just it." Murray hitched an ankle across the other knee and wrapped his long fingers around his shinbone. "I've been patient, I really have. But she just won't believe that you're never coming back to her." Murray's brow crumpled with his frown. "You're not, are you?"

"Hell, no. It's over with Sherry and me."

Murray didn't look encouraged. "She won't give me a chance."

"Murray. What do you want me to say? It's over. I've told her several times. I don't know what more to do."

"She spent last night cryin' on my shoulder over you." Murray glowered at him. "I waited long enough, you know? Months. It's time I got my chance with her. She's…"

"What?"

"I'm telling you straight, Carter. Telling you more than you got any right to know. She's a passionate person, as hotheaded as she is beautiful. I love that about her. I want all that fire directed at me."

Carter put up both hands. "More power to you, buddy. I'm not standing in your way."

"Yeah. Yeah, you are."

"Oh, come on."

"Carter. You are. You're standing between me and my future happiness."

"I don't know what to say to you. Sherry and I broke up a long time ago. It's as over as it gets. I don't see how I can make it any more clear to her."

"Move on, Carter."

"I *have* moved on."

"Choose someone new. As long as you stay unattached, Sherry can tell herself that you're coming back to her and I don't have a prayer of showing her that I'm the man she needs."

Carter shook his head. "I'm sorry, Murray. I can't help you with this. I hope you get through to her. But there's no way I'm up for trying again with someone new anytime soon. As long as we're putting it right out there, Murray, the truth is, I always make a mess of it with women somehow. I'm losing heart, you know? I'm about done."

Murray jumped up. He turned to the side wall and stared at the Prime Sports and Fitness calendar hanging there. November had an image of a gorgeous woman's back and shapely arms as she executed a lat pull on a Universal machine. "Well, how about Paige?" Murray asked without taking his eyes off the calendar.

It took Carter a moment to make sense of Murray's question—and even then, he didn't really understand it. "What do you mean, how about Paige?"

Murray faced him then. "I mean, why the hell don't you just settle down with Paige? Everyone in town can see that you two are meant for each other. And come on, you practically live together already. You sure you're not *already* with Paige and just keeping it a secret for some reason known only to the two of you?"

"Already with Paige? Have you lost your mind, Murray?"

"No, I have not. What I've lost is my heart. To Sherry. I want her to get over you and love me back."

"And I sympathize with that. I would *love* for her to forget about me and be all about you. I've told her it's over more times than I can count. I don't take her calls or answer her texts or her emails. If she drops in on me, I send her away. I've done everything I can to—"

"No. No, you haven't, Carter. You haven't shown it's over by moving on. And if you think about it a little, you'll see I'm right. You and Paige are a great match. And frankly, if you choose Paige, Sherry will definitely wake up and smell the coffee. She's always gone on about Paige, always believed that you're secretly in love with Paige."

Carter made a strangled sound. "Are you crazy? Of course I'm not secretly in love with Paige."

Murray grunted. "Sherry would never admit it, but we both know she sees Paige as the rival she couldn't beat."

"Uh, we do?"

A firm nod from Murray. "You bet we do. So if you and Paige finally get together, finally couple up and admit what's really going on between you, Sherry will have to accept that she's never getting you back."

Carter cleared his throat. "Murray."

"What?"

"I'm sorry, Murray, but no. Just…no."

Murray glared at him. "I'm only asking you to think about it."

"There's nothing to think about."

"What is the matter with you?" Murray practically shouted. "Why can't you see?"

"Murray, whoa. Chill."

But Murray did not chill. "Open your mind, Carter!"

He turned and flung the door open. "Open your mind and see the light." Murray left, slamming the door good and hard behind him.

Carter stared at that door for several very long seconds. And then he shrugged and opened his laptop again and put Murray Preble out of his mind.

Or tried to.

Unfortunately, Murray's weird visit stuck with him, made the Cobra engine schematics blur in front of him, made it so all he could think about was Paige.

"Open your mind!" Murray had yelled at him just before he slammed the office door.

Carter kept thinking about that. About his mind opening.

Opening like a door, a door that hadn't really been there before. He looked through that new open door and saw everything he wanted: marriage and a family.

To a sane and even-tempered woman.

A woman like Paige.

Because Murray was right. Paige was perfect for Carter.

No. Of course, he wasn't in love with Paige. He wasn't in love with anybody. Carter had no intention of going to the stupid place, thank you very much. But now that he'd opened that door, he could clearly see that Paige was just about as good as it got for a man like him.

How come he'd never realized it before?

Paige was smart and fun, and he loved being with her. She was completely reasonable, no drama, not ever. He worked with her and he hung with her and her little sister was family to him. Even their dogs were best friends.

He couldn't imagine his life without Paige. And to marry her and have kids with her…

Hot damn. That could work out. That could be good.

Carter got up from his desk and stared at the fine back and arms of Miss Superfit November as he worked out the kinks in the plan he was formulating.

Kinks like the fact that to have kids together, he and Paige would have to have sex with each other.

That could be weird. He'd never considered sex and Paige in the same sentence before—or wait. Scratch that. He *had* been attracted to Paige way back at the beginning. But then they'd decided to be friends without benefits and he'd accepted that.

So the idea of having sex with her didn't gross him out or leave him cold. It had just always seemed like a bad idea to go there, to take the chance of messing up a great friendship—not to mention a successful business partnership.

However, now that he'd let himself consider the concept of Paige as a bed partner, well, it didn't strike him as awful. He could get into it. He was sure that he could. And sex didn't necessarily have to screw up what they had. If they got married, that would only make their friendship and business partnership stronger.

Oh, yeah. The door was open, all right, open wide and showing him everything. It all fell into place.

He didn't have to be alone. He could get married and have a family, after all.

A family with his best friend.

A family with Paige…

Talk about huge.

Carter left BCC at a quarter after five that night. He'd planned to go home and shower, then take Sally and head over to Paige's.

But after opening that door in his mind and seeing a family with Paige on the other side, well, he wasn't quite ready to spend the evening with her. It was all too new and also a little bit scary.

He had to find just the right way to bring it up to her.

And he needed to find out for sure if they had the necessary physical chemistry together.

And hey. What if she just said no?

Uh-uh. He wasn't ready to see Paige. He could blow this whole thing before it even got started if he didn't handle it right.

So that night he stayed home.

Paige spent the day on household stuff. She bought groceries and baked a casserole, vacuumed and dusted the downstairs.

And the whole day she kind of dreaded the evening, when Carter would show up and she'd have to deal with him while knowing that her sister—and apparently most of the people they knew—believed that Paige was in love with him.

And that he was in love with her.

Awkward. Embarrassing. Too strange for words.

She hardly knew what to say to him—to Carter, of all people.

But then, as it turned out, he didn't show up.

And that just made her sad. So she put on some old yoga pants and a baggy sweatshirt, streamed a tearjerker on Netflix and ate a quart of Ben & Jerry's Chunky Monkey.

The next morning, Sunday, Carter considered chickening out again and not showing up at Paige's to walk Biscuit with Sally, not being there to get the coffee going.

But if he bailed on their usual routine again, he'd have to admit to himself that opening the door in his mind had freaked him out just a little—hell. Who was he kidding?

Opening that door freaked him out a *lot*.

But freaking out was no excuse to turn wimp and bail on his girls.

So he walked Biscuit with Sally as usual and then let himself back into Paige's quiet house and made the coffee.

He was standing at the fridge, staring inside, trying to decide what to make for breakfast as his brain kept insisting on circling back to the mind-altering concept of Paige and him and a houseful of baby Bravos, when he heard a soft sigh behind him.

A hot bolt of lightning seemed to surge across his shoulder blades and the hair on the back of his neck stood to attention. Bizarre.

He shut the door and turned around.

And there she was: Paige, leaning in the doorway, wearing that old plaid robe, flannel pajamas and silly fuzzy slippers he'd seen a hundred times. She'd tried to comb her hair, but she must have slept on it hard, because it still stuck up on the left side.

"Hey," she said. The single huskily spoken word seemed to hit him in the chest and then curl around him like a hug.

"Mornin'." Damn, she was cute. With those big brown eyes and that soft, pretty mouth. Not aggressively sexy, not showy like most of the women he'd dated. But hot in her own down-to-earth, *real* sort of way. The more he looked at her, the more he thought he could definitely tap that.

And wouldn't it be great to live here with her in the house she grew up in, to stop going back and forth between their houses? Her house was homier than his, a perfect place to raise their family.

If she would have him.

She was so smart. And she could be intimidating with that steady, unruffled way she had of looking at a guy. Since that bastard in college broke her heart, she didn't give her trust easily—not to men, anyway.

But he had a head start on that, being her best friend and all.

"What?" She straightened in the doorway.

"Nothing." It came out nice and calm, giving zero hint of the nervous energy churning inside him. "I was thinking eggs Benedict. I didn't make muffins, but I see you have some store-bought."

"Sounds wonderful." She went to the coffeepot and filled a mug, turning back around the way she did almost every morning, leaning on the counter for her first sip. A pleasured sound escaped her.

Would she make sounds like that in bed?

He realized he really wanted to find out.

The big brown eyes were soft and shadowed. He couldn't really read them. She said, "You're good to us, Carter. Thank you."

"I never did anything I didn't want to do." It came out gruff, low. It wasn't what he'd meant to say and he wondered where the hell it came from.

But those soft lips turned up in the beginning of a smile. "I know that."

"I like it here, with you. With Dawn."

"I'm glad."

He was maybe three steps away from her. It would have been so easy, to close the distance, take the mug, set it on the counter. Draw her into his arms…

"Carter, hey!" Dawn chirped from the doorway, shattering the moment. She joined him at the fridge, pulling the door open again and taking out a carton of orange juice. "What's for breakfast?"

"Eggs Benedict," said Paige.

"Yum. Just what I was I hoping for." Dawn edged around Carter, set the pitcher on the counter and opened the cupboard to get down the juice glasses.

Paige and Dawn got the table ready and he cooked the food. They sat down to eat. Things started getting really strange about then. He kept having the feeling that something was going on at that table between the sisters, as if they knew something he didn't and both of them were on edge about it.

They told him repeatedly, way more times than necessary, how much they loved his eggs Benedict. Then they started in on Christmas stuff—on how they were looking forward to Rocky Mountain Christmas, Justice Creek's big holiday shopping event next Saturday.

Next Saturday was also the date of the Holiday Ball at Justice Creek's world-famous Haltersham Hotel. It was a charity event to support the local children's shelter. Carter had bought a bunch of tickets at a chamber of commerce auction months ago and passed them out at the shop. He'd given some to Dawn and Paige, as well. At the time, he'd planned to take Sherry. When they broke up, he'd gotten Paige to agree to go with him.

He asked Dawn, "So, are you going to use those tickets I gave you for the Holiday Ball?"

She nodded. "Me and Molly and a couple of other friends are going together."

"Sounds good." He turned to Paige. "We still on for that?"

Her eyes looked enormous suddenly. She stammered out, "Uh, yeah. Sure. Of course, we are."

Dawn chimed in way too brightly, "I think it's going to be cool!"

Paige started talking again—as if she couldn't get away from the subject of the ball fast enough. Suddenly, she was all about how she needed to bring the Christmas stuff down from the attic. Dawn said she wanted to go to Molly's after breakfast, but she promised that later in the day, she'd come back and help with hauling the boxes down, and then they could maybe start on the tree.

Carter said, "I'll bring it all down for you, soon as we're through with breakfast." All the girlie chatter ceased abruptly. He looked at Paige and then at Dawn and then back at Paige again. "What did I say?"

"Nothing," said Dawn.

"You *didn't*," added Paige. "You didn't say a thing."

None of this made sense. They kept shooting each other looks. "What's going on here?"

"Nothing, really," Paige insisted. She and Dawn traded frantic glances that told him there was actually a whole lot going on here.

Women. He knew he had to give it up, that if they didn't want to tell him, he was never going to know.

He shrugged. "So, then…I'll get the Christmas stuff down before I go?"

"Um, great," said Dawn.

"Thank you," said Paige. "I'll help. It won't take long."

After the meal, he cleared off while Paige and Dawn ran upstairs to get dressed. Paige came down a few minutes later in jeans and an old flannel shirt, her hair tied up in a ponytail. He followed her back up to the attic, admiring the view the whole way. She filled out those worn jeans real nice.

At the top of the stairs, she hustled along the landing to the door at the end where a narrow set of steps led up to the area under the eaves. They went up. Paige pulled the chain on the bulb that hung from the rafters, and light filled the dusty space.

"Over here." She pointed at the stacks of plastic bins and cardboard boxes grouped together near the one small attic window that looked out the front of the house. Her eight-foot tree was there, in three sections, wrapped in heavy plastic for protection.

They went to work hauling everything down to the living room. It took several trips up and back. The whole time, he kept on the lookout for his moment—to try a first kiss, maybe.

Or to catch her arm, turn her toward him, tell her that he had something important to say…

But somehow the moment never came. She seemed in a really big hurry. And she actively avoided meeting his eyes. Whenever they happened to face each other in the process of turning to the stairs or grabbing for another box, her gaze would slide on by, not once connecting with his.

When he set the last bin down in the living room, she suddenly couldn't get rid of him fast enough.

"Whew." She gave him a blinding smile, at the same time letting her gaze skitter away to some point past his left shoulder. "That was easy. Thanks to you—and you're excused, Carter. I've got it from here."

Excused.

He was *excused*?

What did that even mean? Excused for the day? For freaking ever?

Forget it. He wasn't even going to ask. Instead, he suggested, "How about you let me help you get the tree upright before I go?"

For that, he got a blinding smile, one that seemed more than a little forced. "That would be great…"

So she grabbed the stand and set it up, centering it in the bay window that faced the front yard. They peeled the protective wrapping off the tree sections and she guided them into place as he lowered them.

After that, he figured she could manage the rest. And by then, he couldn't wait to get out of there. He called Sally in from the kitchen, took her leash and his jacket from the hook by the door—and left.

At home, he kind of settled down a little. He started thinking that he'd let his nervousness about approaching Paige as a woman—as a prospective bride, for crying out loud—affect his judgment.

There was nothing going on with Paige. Or with Dawn, either. He was the one with the problem. He felt edgy and unsure. He didn't know how to kick-start a conversation about forever—not with Paige. He'd never expected to be talking about marriage with her.

He needed more time to think about it. Too bad that thinking about it, so far, had gotten him exactly nowhere.

One thing for certain, though, he'd lose what was left of his mind if he spent the day hanging around the house. So he went on over to BCC, which was closed on Sunday.

Alone in the deserted shop, he played heavy metal at mind-numbing volume and went to work bolting the stupid spoiler to the trunk of Deacon's Cobra.

* * *

Paige had the Christmas carols playing and was arranging strings of lighted garland on the mantel when Dawn and Molly came in at noon. The girls made grilled cheese sandwiches and heated up a couple of cans of soup, then called Paige in to join them.

After lunch, Molly and Dawn pitched in with the tree and the other decorations. It was nice, really, with the holiday tunes playing and the three of them humming along, dragging Christmas treasures out of the boxes and bins and hanging them on the tree.

Molly, fuller-figured than Paige, with thick black hair and big dark eyes, spent so much time at their house she counted as a sister, too. Her parents had divorced the year before and Molly said she felt more at home with the Kettleman sisters than she did at her mom's house or at the condo where her dad lived with his new girlfriend. Paige and Dawn had taken care to stay on good terms with both of Molly's parents, so her folks had no issue with Molly hanging at Dawn's a lot of the time.

It was lovely, that Sunday afternoon, a holiday memory in the making—Dawn and Molly and Paige, getting the house ready for the holidays. Really, life lately was just about perfect.

Or it would be, if not for Paige's problem with Carter. Since the damn love quiz, she found it hard even to talk to him. She felt so nervous around him.

And it hurt him, the way she was behaving. She could see the confusion and pain in his eyes. He didn't know what was wrong. He didn't understand.

And she didn't know what to do about that.

Hold steady and wait? Only six days had passed since

that day at Deacon Leery's office. She couldn't help hoping that maybe this crazy feeling would fade.

Or maybe honesty was the best policy. Maybe she should just...bust herself to him. Tell him she was in love with him and let the chips fall where they may.

Paige cringed at the thought. How could that possibly go well? The man couldn't get away fast enough when women started using the *L* word around him.

And surely it was too early for such a drastic move.

Dear God. This was *hard.*

Why now? It didn't even seem fair.

She'd finally gotten over her parents' deaths—or as over it as a person ever gets after something like that. She loved her job and business was good. Her sister was happy, graduating with honors in the spring. She had Carter for companionship. And now and then, she went out with attractive men, but refused to get bogged down in the responsibilities of a committed relationship.

Everything was just right.

Until this.

"You need to go talk to him," Dawn said.

Paige realized she was standing at the tree, staring blankly into space, a misshapen clay star she'd made in second grade dangling from one hand.

Molly, hanging a crystal snowflake from a high branch, nodded in agreement with Dawn. Paige realized that Dawn must have told her about the love quiz.

Which was okay with Paige. If you couldn't trust your honorary other sister, well, who could you trust? And Molly was every bit as respectful of a confidence as Dawn.

Paige hung the ugly ornament, tucking it in among the branches where it wouldn't be too obvious. "Funny,

I love the ugly ones as much as the pretty ones. Each one is a memory, precious. To be treasured, you know?" Tears blurred her vision. She dashed them away.

And Dawn said, "I mean it, Paige. Go!"

A sad little whimper escaped her. "You think? Really?"

"Yes, I do," Dawn declared.

"He's probably at the shop—"

"Go," Dawn commanded again.

Paige freshened up a little, put on minimal makeup and changed into red skinny jeans, ankle boots and a raglan-sleeved red sweater over a tan tank.

Dawn was waiting at the door, holding her coat.

Fifteen minutes later, she pulled her SUV in next to Carter's dually at BCC.

Would he be annoyed with her for butting in on his private time with his latest four-wheeled baby?

Too bad.

Dawn was right. Paige needed to talk to him. Needed to tell him…

What?

Better not think about that. If she started thinking, she'd never get out of the car.

She shoved open her door and jumped out, taking off at a run for the shop's side entrance. She could hear hard rock blaring, even through the thick walls and steel door.

He'd left it unlocked. She pushed the door wide. The loud music got louder. She hesitated on the threshold, but only for a second. Then, on shaky legs, she went in, pausing to shut the door gently and turn the lock, too.

The shop went dead quiet.

She whirled back around just in time to see Carter toss the stereo remote onto a workbench.

"Paige." His voice was so rough, but in the most delicious way. He wore old jeans, a black tee and an ancient navy blue hoodie. And he had a black smudge in the middle of his forehead. Had any man on earth ever looked so hot?

Nope. Never. Not in the whole history of humankind.

And the way he stared at her—as if he'd missed her, as if he hadn't seen her in years.

Sparks flashed across the surface of her skin from that look in his eyes. He looked…determined somehow.

What in the world was happening here?

And then he started moving, started coming toward her across the concrete floor. Coming *for* her, with…

Could that possibly be desire in his eyes?

Please. She must be dreaming. She blinked several times in rapid succession, to wake herself up.

But she didn't wake up. And by then, well, if this was a dream, she hoped she *wouldn't* wake up. Because Carter still had all that thrilling fire in his eyes and he kept coming until he was standing right in front of her.

She gasped as he reached out to cradle her face between his big strong oil-smudged hands. "Paige."

And then he kissed her.

Chapter Four

Dear sweet Lord in heaven.

He smelled so good. Like gasoline and the air right before a thunderstorm. Gasoline and ozone and something else, too, something so very Carter it made her heart ache.

His big hands were rough and warm against her cold cheeks. Amazing, that kiss. Those firm, hot lips of his at first gentle, nudging, brushing…

And then pressing harder as her own mouth gave to him, opening, letting him in.

His tongue. Rough and soft and hot and slippery. It swept the inner surfaces of her mouth, slid in between her upper lip and her teeth, tasting her, *knowing* her.

There was a groan. Hers? His? She really couldn't tell.

Wherever that low, purring sound came from, it echoed deliciously inside her head as his fingers threaded upward, combing through the hair at her temples, tracing the shape of her ear. Oh, those fingers. They caused a series of shivers like hot, fierce electric shocks to arc across her scalp.

Another groan. That one had definitely come from her own throat, the sound rising from the center of her, all quivery with need.

And still, he kept kissing her, touching her so lightly, running those rough fingers down the sides of her throat, around the back of her neck, clasping her, holding her in place.

So that he could kiss her some more.

Breathless, she was, dizzy with the wonder and the heat of it. Had there ever, in the history of time, been such a slow, hot kiss as this one?

Their first real kiss…

My God.

Imagine that.

Her knees were actually trembling. She had the strangest sensation of falling. At the same time, she was soaring. And his mouth just kept on playing with hers.

She managed to lift her own two hands and grab on to his big rock-hard forearms. That was the only way she kept herself from slithering to the concrete floor, just melting downward, knees collapsing, into a quaking puddle of wonder, confusion and lust.

It ended from overload. The pleasure, the wonder, the total disbelief that this could be happening between her and Carter…

It all swirled together until her head was reeling and her knees were knocking.

With a soft, lost cry, she broke the kiss and swayed against him.

"Paige…" He whispered her name as he gathered her in, those bulging arms of his holding on, holding her up.

With a sigh, she let her head fall against his big chest. "I can't believe…"

He chuckled, the sound vibrating thrillingly against her ear. "What?"

"You. And me…" She took a minute to breathe. Just breathe. His scent was all around her, that wonderful smell of rain and heat and axle grease. "Can't be happening…"

"Oh, it's happening." He caught her chin and tipped her face up so she had to look at him. He was so beautiful. Moss-green eyes, finely cut cheekbones, thick, scruffy hair. And that mouth…

Oh, my. That mouth…

He rubbed at her cheek with his thumb. "I got grease on you. Sorry."

Like she even cared. "It's okay. It's fine, really…"

He looked at her so hungrily, a look that made her face feel hot and the core of her feel heavy and lazy and ready for anything. "But I had to do that," he said. "I had to kiss you."

She stared up at him, drinking him in with her eyes—drunk on him, really. Her mind felt so slow, so foolish and thick. "Uh, you did? You *had* to kiss me?"

"Yeah." Beneath the scruff on his lean cheeks, a muscle twitched. "And I'm *glad* I did."

Her heart beat faster. With happiness. With hope. "Yeah?"

He had that determined look again. "Paige, there's something I need to talk to you about."

At that, her heart bounced skyward and got caught in her throat. She swallowed hard to make it drop back into her chest where it belonged. “Ahem. Um. Sure. Yeah. Go for it.”

He took her by the shoulders and set her gently away, all the while holding her there with his eyes. “I'll just wash my hands. We can go in my office.”

“This is starting to sound kind of scary…”

His still held her in place with those big hands. “You're looking a little freaked. You're not going bolt on me, are you?”

“Of course not.” It was just that, well, she'd come to talk to *him*. And now suddenly *he* had to talk to *her*? What about? She forced a trembling smile. “Go on. Wash up. I'll wait right here.”

He gave her shoulders one final squeeze and then he went to the metal closet next to the concrete sink in the corner. He took off the hoodie and hung it in the closet. She watched the broad, powerful muscles of his back shift beneath the black T-shirt as he flipped on the taps, soaped up and rinsed his hands and then washed his face and neck, too.

When he came back to her, the T-shirt was wet at the neck and he smelled of borax and Joy dishwashing soap, the familiar combination they used in the shop to get the engine grease off without taking the skin, too. That smell, so familiar, made her suddenly teary-eyed. Borax and Joy and all the years that she and Carter had been friends.

From casual friends. To good friends. To best friends. It had been a natural development, an almost imperceptible progression. Over time, they grew closer, their lives meshing at home and here at BCC.

She really liked being his best friend.

But all of that would change now, which scared her to death and broke her heart, too.

"You okay?" He stood right in front of her again, so big and strong and hot and beautiful. No wonder his women always ended up falling too hard. The old T-shirt fit him like a second skin. She could see the heavily cut musculature of his shoulders and chest, see those washboard abs. She could see all the things about him that she'd never really paid much attention to until recently. The *male* things, the things that now made her want him way more than could possibly be wise.

"Paige?"

She shook herself. "I'm fine. Yeah."

He lifted a hand—slowly, as though he feared he might spook her—and he guided her hair back from her face on one side, following the long strands down, smoothing them over her shoulder. An encouraging smile pulled at those lips she really wanted to kiss again. "My office?"

"Sure."

He let his fingers trail down her arm to clasp her hand. And then he pulled her along with him, across the shop to the inner door.

His office had the basics: desk, laptop, guest chair, file cabinet. And an ugly brown corduroy sofa on one wall. He dropped to the sofa and pulled her down next to him.

"See, it all started with Murray Preble." He eased one big arm along the sofa back and hitched a knee up to the cushions.

She took off her coat and didn't know what to do with it, so she tossed it across the sofa arm. "Murray the auto parts guy?"

"Yep." His bronze eyebrows drew together. "But first, there was Sherry."

Paige sat up a little straighter when he said his old girlfriend's name. "What about Sherry?"

He raked his spiky hair back with his fingers. "You were out of it when that happened."

"Out of it? Excuse me?"

"Don't get all prickly. It was last week. Black Friday. When you were in Denver with Nell and Jody and having those hormone problems, remember?"

She reminded herself not to get annoyed with him for bringing up hormone problems, the way men always did. After all, she'd *told* him it was hormones. "Right. I remember."

"I wanted to tell you all this sooner, but you haven't been talking to me—or even wanting me around."

She felt contrite then, she really did. "I am sorry, Carter. That I haven't been available, that we haven't talked."

"It's okay." He looked at her so steadily. "We're past it, right?"

She gave him a shy smile. "Yeah. We are. Totally past it."

He was staring at her mouth. "I really want to kiss you again." And his gaze shifted up to meet her waiting eyes. "You better stop looking at me like that. It's way too distracting."

A wave of sweet pleasure washed through her. He wanted to kiss her. *Wow.* This could be good. Really, really good. "Sorry." She tried her best to look unkissable. "Go on. It was on Black Friday..."

"Yeah. I was here, in the shop, working out the kinks

in Terrence Bolger's '61 Lincoln Continental. Sherry showed up..."

He went on to tell her all about Sherry in her thong and Santa hat and killer high heels. Paige ignored the twinge of jealousy as he related the story. Sherry Leland was drop-dead gorgeous. But Paige knew Carter. He'd been over Sherry for a long time now. She even felt a little sad for the other woman when Carter told her how he'd put Sherry's coat back on her and sent her on her way.

Carter continued. "Then on Saturday, Murray comes by. He wants a private word with me. Turns out, he's in love with Sherry and he wants me to find another girlfriend. He said that if I found someone new, Sherry would finally have to accept that it was over between her and me."

Paige couldn't help scoffing. "Murray wants Sherry, so *you're* supposed to find another girlfriend. Just like that?"

Carter grunted. "Exactly. I told him no."

"Of course you did."

"He got a little worked up. And then he started talking about you."

"Hold on. What have *I* got to do with anything?"

Carter eyed her sideways. "Don't get pissed off, now."

"I'm not. I'm also not following. Could you just answer my question, please?"

"Fine. Murray said I ought to get together with you."

Her throat clutched. "Um. With me?"

"That's right. He said that you should be my girlfriend. He said everyone in town knows that you and me are meant for each other."

Oh. My. Golly. Weakly, she asked, "They do?" She

couldn't believe it. Murray had told Carter what Dawn had told *her*, that everyone "knew" about her and Carter—except her and Carter.

Carter nodded. "According to Murray, you and me have a secret thing going on—so secret, we don't even know about it ourselves. According to Murray, Sherry has always felt that you're the one rival for my, er, affections that she could never beat."

"Wow." So there really was hope, then, for the two of them, maybe? Cautiously, she asked him, "So...what did you say then?"

Another grunt from Carter. "What do you think? I told Murray *again* that I'm not getting a new girlfriend just so that he can have a better shot with Sherry."

"Of course you're not," she echoed numbly, all her bright, shiny new hopes dying a thousand deaths. "That would be a really bad reason to start a new relationship."

"Because I don't *want* a new relationship."

Pull yourself together, Kettleman. It's not his fault if he's not interested.

But then, why had he *kissed* her?

Why had he said she made him want to kiss her *again*?

He was looking worried all of a sudden. "Er, Paige? You still with me?"

She drew her shoulders back. "Of course. I'm right here. I heard every word and...well, okay, then. That's settled."

Twin lines formed between his eyebrows. "What's settled?"

"That you're not just getting some girl to go out with because Murray can't stand the competition."

"Damn straight I'm not. But Murray did get me thinking..."

"Ah." She tried to appear interested in the usual best-friend sort of way. "Thinking about...?"

"You. And me."

"Wait a minute. You and me? What do you mean, you and me?"

He was staring off toward the fitness calendar on the far wall. "I wish I could describe it, Paige. It was like a door, you know? A door opening up in my mind."

"I am just not following."

"A door that swung wide...and there you were."

"Me?"

"Yeah. You. And it, well, it just hit me, you know?"

"What hit you?"

"What I want, what I've been looking for all this time...it's you."

A strange, squeaky sound escaped her. "Er, me?"

"I have a proposal, Paige."

This was all so very confusing. "I don't...what?"

"Just listen. Just let me explain."

"I...okay. All right, Carter. You go ahead, why don't you? You go ahead and explain."

Carter jumped up so suddenly that she gasped. She stared up over his lean hips and the very tempting hint of package displayed by the frayed zipper of his jeans. She took in his corrugated abs and broad chest so lovingly outlined by that old T-shirt. She skimmed his big shoulders, his thick, powerful neck, let her gaze track on up, until she was looking directly into his shining green eyes.

That was when he said, "I want us to get engaged."

Paige swallowed. Hard. "Engaged in what?"

"*Engaged*, Paige. As in 'to be married.' I want us to get engaged right now, today, and I want us to get married within a few months. I want to move into your house with you and Dawn. Because I want to be together with you—really together. Completely together. And that means marriage. That means children. That means a family, Paige. I want us to make a family."

Somehow she managed to sputter out, "But I don't—"

He cut her off, with enthusiasm. "Open your *mind*, Paige." He dropped to the couch again and took her chin in his big borax-scented hand. "Just open your mind and you'll see that it's perfect, *you're* perfect." He said it so tenderly her heart kind of melted. "And you've been right there in the center of my life for so long now."

"Oh, Carter…"

"You're everything I want in a woman. You've got heart, Paige. And a great sense of humor. You're good at math. Easy on the eyes…" He let go of her chin, but he didn't stop talking. "You're sane and smart and reasonable."

"Uh, thank you. I think."

"There's never going to be any big emo drama with you because I'm not in love with you and you're not in love with me."

There. That. All wrong. Not surprising, not in the least, coming from Carter. But all wrong for her.

Because she *was* in love with him. Desperately, damn it.

And he was still talking. "We're best friends, plain and simple. And who better for any guy to marry than his best friend?"

"Well, Carter, I…"

"You what?" He scrunched up his forehead at her, as though *she* were the one saying crazy things.

She suggested gingerly, "Well, you have to see that this is pretty out there, what you're suggesting, don't you think?"

"Out there? No. Not in the least. Yeah, I was a little bit concerned that we might not have any sexual chemistry given that, until now, it's never occurred to either of us to even fool around a little, when we're together practically 24/7. But hey. Now I've kissed you. I think we can both agree that the chemistry thing won't be a problem." Paige opened her mouth to say…she had no idea what. And he just went cheerfully on. "Paige. Really. I get that this is a lot to take in."

"You do, huh?"

"What is that? Sarcasm? Come on, Paige. How 'bout this? You think about it for a day or two, okay?"

"A *day* or two?"

"Yeah, that ought to be long enough, right?"

"But I—"

"Paige. I have one important point left to make to you."

"Ah. Well. Good to know."

"And my point is this…" He reached across the cushion between them, pulled her close and kissed her again, those amazing lips of his settling on hers so perfectly, his clever tongue delving in, his big arms all hard and hot around her.

Wow! Who knew just kissing could feel like this?

She'd been missing out big-time on the sex front, that was for sure.

When he finally lifted that amazing mouth off hers and grinned down at her, her head was spinning.

She told him so. "Carter. My head is spinning."

"What'd I tell you? Chemistry." That wonderful mouth swooped toward her again.

"Stop." She brought up her hands and pressed them flat to his rock-hard chest.

"Stop?" He looked hurt. "I thought you said you *liked* kissing me."

She resisted the urge to reach up and tenderly lay her palm along the side of his too-handsome face. "I do like kissing you."

"Well, then, what's the—?"

"I have things to say and I can't say them while you're making my head spin with your incredible kisses."

He let her go then. And he looked way too pleased with himself. "Incredible? My kisses are incredible?"

"Yes." She did her best to look stern. "Now, can we move on, please?"

He flopped back to his end of the ugly couch, stretching that big arm along the couch back again. "Yeah. Shoot."

She tried hard to order her thoughts—no mean feat when he looked at her as though he'd like to gobble her up for lunch. "I think we need to slow this down a little."

He shook his head. "No. Bad idea. What we need is—"

"Stop." She showed him the hand. "Listen. *I'm* talking now."

"Sorry." The gleam in his eyes said he really wasn't sorry in the least.

She proceeded before he could start in again. "I think you're really rushing this and there's no reason to rush."

"Wrong."

"Am I speaking or not?" she asked sharply.

He made a disgruntled sound, but then allowed, "Go ahead."

She did, quickly, before he could run over her some more. "Why can't we just slow down a little? Let's just, you know, go out together, like people do. *Be* together like two normal human beings. We can take it one day at a time, and see how it goes. Why do we have to get instantly *engaged*, for heaven's sake?"

He grinned his cocky, way-too-charming grin. "You know me, Paige. Go big. Or go home. I'm thirty-four years old. Now that I know what I want, I don't want to waste another day. I want to get going on this—and here's a thought. How about you just look at it as sort of a test-drive engagement, if that makes you feel better?"

"A *what*?"

"A test drive," he said, clearly tickled pink at the thought. "We'll test each other out, get a solid sense for whether or not we want to seal the deal."

"You can't be serious. Did you *have* to make a car analogy at a time like this?"

Those fabulous shoulders lifted in a lazy shrug. "Say you'll marry me, and we'll be together—I mean, *really* together—through the holidays. We'll let the whole town know that we're engaged. Then on New Year's Day we'll evaluate the situation and decide if we want to say I do."

"Evaluate?" Surely he hadn't actually said that.

Oh, but he had. "Yeah. Evaluate. You know, the way you always make me do when we have to come to a decision for BCC. We'll make a list of pros and cons and see which side is longer."

"Carter. I have to ask. What planet *are* you from?"

"Okay, yeah. It sounds a little crazy, I know."

"Crazy is too sane a word."

"I'm thirty-four, Paige."

"You said that already."

"And I'll say it again. I'm thirty-four and I want a family. And I've finally realized that you're the one I want my family with. I want to get moving on that. I see no reason at all for us to drag our feet—plus, hey. We'll be helping Murray out in the bargain. Now come back here." He reached for her again. She should have resisted. But somehow, well, it just felt so good when he put his arms around her.

"Don't you dare," she whispered, but it was really hard to mean it when she was all wrapped up in his embrace, feeling breathless—and suddenly yearning.

His lips were only an inch from hers. "Come on, Paige." He was so big and solid and he smelled so good. "It's just a kiss."

"I don't—"

"Just one?" he coaxed, all sweet and charming now. "Please?"

Somehow her hand had slid up to clasp the back of his neck. Her fingers brushed the blunt ends of his hair. "Oh, Carter…"

"Yeah?" His eyes were tender now, golden light gleaming within the green.

"Maybe just one…" She tightened her grip on the back of his neck. He let her do that, let her pull him down to her, until his mouth covered hers.

She moaned at the contact. He made a low, rumbling, satisfied sound in response.

His big hands roamed her back, and his hot tongue invaded her willing mouth.

Why, oh, why, did he have to be so good at kissing? It wasn't fair. No wonder the women who fell for him always had trouble letting him go. He got them all sexed up until they couldn't think of anything but his big hands and that plump mouth, so soft and pliant in comparison to the rest of him.

He lifted that mouth a fraction, whispered her name, "Paige…" and slanted his kiss the other way. She moaned again and his hands slid down to cup both cheeks of her bottom.

It felt so good, his hands holding her, palms spread, fingers digging in, his mouth taking hers. She lifted herself toward him, pressing her body closer, harder…

Really. Truly. This *had* to stop.

Gathering every ounce of will she possessed, she shoved him away again and scooted back to her side of the sofa.

"Paige, what the hell?" he demanded, rough and low.

They stared at each other across the width of the center cushion, both of them breathing raggedly. A hot flush burned on his cheeks, and his eyes were green fire.

She got up fast, before he could reach for her again. "Look, I…I don't know what to say."

But he did. "Say yes."

She smoothed her hair, tugged on her sweater, then snatched up her coat from the end of the couch. "I can't do this right now."

"When, then?" He growled the question.

"I…I don't know. Really, Carter. It's all too much. I have to go. We'll talk about this later."

"But when?"

"I don't know. A few days. I…need to think."

He started to say something else but then seemed to change his mind. He sprawled back against the cushions, all big and handsome and way too manly. "There's no point in running away, Paige. You have to know that."

Maybe not. But right at the moment, running away seemed like the only option.

She whirled and got out of there before he could try again to stop her—before she could weaken and admit to herself that all she wanted to do was stay.

Chapter Five

Dawn and Molly were putting the last ornaments on the tree when Paige got back to the house. Pentatonix sang "Mary, Did You Know?" in perfect harmony from the living room speaker dock.

Paige hung her coat in the front closet. Biscuit appeared, wriggling in ecstasy at the sight of her. She bent down and gave him a nice rub around the collar. He followed her to the open arch between the living room and the front hall, where she paused to admire the girls' work. "You two have a gift. It looks so beautiful."

Dawn got right to the real question. "What happened? Was he there?"

"Oh, yeah."

"And?"

"Ugh." Paige headed for the sofa, where she dropped to the cushions. "I cannot even tell you." She planted her face in her hands. With a whine of sympathy, Biscuit dropped to his haunches at her feet. Both girls ran to her. They nudged Biscuit out of the way and sat on either side of her, each throwing an arm around her so they shared a group hug.

Dawn asked, "Bad?"

Paige pulled her face out of her hands. "I just… I can't talk about it now."

Molly asked, "But are we *mad* at him?"

Dawn chimed in with "Molly's right. We need to know whether to yell at him or ignore him the next time we see him."

In spite of all the strong emotions roiling inside her, Paige couldn't help chuckling. "No, we're not mad at him. We're not ignoring him. We're not yelling at him—well, *I* might, eventually. But not you two. He hasn't done anything bad. Much."

"Well, now. There's a mixed signal," Dawn groused.

Paige hooked an arm around her sister's neck and kissed her cheek. "Just treat him like you always treat him. Remember, he loves you and he's always been good to us."

"But did he *reject* you?" Molly demanded.

"Far from it."

Both girls brightened. Dawn said, "So…it's good, then? You two are going to be together?"

"I don't know what's going to happen yet. I really, truly don't. You're going to have to let Carter and me work this out between ourselves."

"No fair." Dawn made a show of sticking out her lower lip. "I want details."

"Well, you're not going to get them. Just believe me when I say you don't have to worry. I'm okay, really. Carter and I are…just fine." Sort of. Maybe. "And I just want you to continue treating him the way you always have." She wrapped an arm around each of them and gave them both a squeeze. "Please?"

Reluctantly, they agreed.

An hour later, the empty boxes and bins were stacked in the front hall, ready to be stowed upstairs again until it was time to put everything away after the holidays. Dawn and Molly had a date with Molly's mom for Sunday dinner, after which the two girls would do homework and practice their music together. They gave Paige more hugs as they left for the house around the block where Molly had grown up.

Once they were gone, the place seemed too quiet. Not so great to be left all alone with nothing but her thoughts for company. She should fix herself dinner.

But she just didn't feel up to cooking right then. So she started hauling the boxes back up to the attic, Biscuit at her heels.

The doorbell chimed as she was coming down for the third time. At the sound, she got that butterflies-in-the-belly feeling. It might be Carter. He usually showed up for dinner Sunday night. And, except in the mornings when he walked the dogs before she got up and often came back and made breakfast, he always respected her privacy and rang the bell.

Definitely him. She could see the sleeve of his black leather jacket through the left sidelight. Sally peered in on the other side, tongue lolling, tail wagging. Biscuit scuttled right over there and sniffed excitedly at the bottom of the door.

Was she tempted not to answer? Definitely. She really wasn't ready to deal with him again.

But she longed to lay eyes on him. If felt like forever

since she'd last seen him, last kissed him, last felt those strong arms around her…

Oh, she had it bad. And really, how could that be good? She wanted his love—and he thought a test-drive engagement was a superfine idea.

Head up and shoulders back, she opened the door.

What do you know? The man of her dreams: Carter, big, bemuscled and hot as ever, dressed all in black, holding an extralarge Romano's pizza. "I come in peace." His hair was still damp from his shower and he'd actually shaved. "Got plans for dinner?"

She muttered defensively, "I was going to figure something out."

"But you haven't yet." He held out the box and the delicious smell grew stronger. "Sausage and mushrooms. Your favorite."

Sally slithered around her as Biscuit chuffed a happy greeting. "Your dog's already in. I guess I have to be nice and let you in, too."

He gave her that grin, the one that made women's panties spontaneously combust. "You want the pizza, you have to put up with me. Package deal."

"Why is it that everything good seems to come with conditions?" She stepped back and gestured him in.

"Dawn?" he asked as he handed her the pizza.

"She's at Molly's till ten."

He hung his jacket on the peg by the door. Underneath, he wore a black, long-sleeved Henley. He shoved the sleeves up those fine corded forearms and tipped his head at the empty Christmas boxes stacked by the stairs. "You want these put away before we eat?"

She was trying so hard to think bad things about him.

But no, he just had to be his usual thoughtful, generous, helpful self. Too bad he was also a man who never really let his girlfriends get all that close, a guy who came up with totally out-there ideas like a test-drive engagement.

"Thank you," she said sweetly. "Getting these boxes to the attic would be wonderful."

"So stash the pizza and let's get after it."

She took the pizza into the kitchen and left it on the snack bar, then rejoined him in the front hall, where she found him leaning in the arch to the living room, one hand stuck in a back pocket. "The tree looks great."

She went and stood beside him. "Yeah. It's that time of year again..."

Now he was watching her. "You're a sucker for Christmas."

"My mom was, too." Paige tried not to stare too long at his mouth, tried not to think of how fine it felt locked on to hers. "My mom collected every last decoration and ornament we ever made in school."

"And you still have them all."

"Oh, yes, I do." The glance they shared had gone on for way too long.

Finally, he said softly, having heard all this before, "And you miss her most this time of year."

"Yeah." Her last memories of her parents were of that final Christmas. They did all the best Christmas things that year, cut down a live tree, made dozens of cookies and way too much divinity and fudge. They'd decked the house up right. There was snow. They all went sledding. "I can still see us, the four of us and Granny Kettleman." Granny had died two years later. "I see us all sitting around the candlelit table in the dining room for

Christmas dinner, holding hands as Granny says grace. In my memories, it's all so perfectly corny and wonderful, like one of those old Norman Rockwell paintings."

Actually, her then-fiancé, Jim Kellogg, had been there that Christmas, too. But somehow, in her memories, she'd managed to blot that jerk right out of the picture.

That year, Paige and Jim had gone back to school two days before New Year's. A week later, her folks went skiing for their anniversary, just the two of them. Dawn had stayed with Molly's family so Mom and Dad could have a special romantic getaway…

Carter's hand brushed her shoulder. "Hey."

She blinked and brought herself back to the moment, to Bing Crosby singing softly in the background, to the Christmas lights on the tree in the bay window. Carter's finger brushed up and down the side of her neck.

Shivers sparked and burned where he touched her. She shouldn't encourage him. Still, it seemed the most natural thing to step in closer. He tipped up her chin with his thumb and lowered his lips to hers.

Paige sighed when his mouth touched hers in a beautiful, sweet kiss. A kiss of comfort and understanding, with just a hint of fire beneath the careful tenderness.

Too soon, he lifted his head. "So. The boxes?"

She nodded. "The boxes. Please."

Once the work was done, they headed for the kitchen. Carter put down fresh kibble for the dogs and then they took the pizza and some beers into the living room. She flipped the switch beside the fireplace and cheery flames licked the fake logs.

They shucked off their boots and got comfy on the sofa, the pizza box open on the coffee table in front of them. He grabbed the remote and turned on the in-progress Broncos game.

Half an hour later, after two fourth-quarter touchdowns, the Broncos were a game up on San Diego in the division race and the giant pizza was all but decimated.

"'Nother beer?" she offered, feeling pretty good about the evening, really. If she didn't let herself think about his outrageous proposal and smoking-hot kisses of that afternoon, she could almost pretend that they were back to the way they'd always been, Carter and Paige, best friends forever.

He nodded. "'Nother beer would be good."

So she took the empties to the kitchen, returning with two fresh ones. She set his on the coffee table in front of him and dropped to her end of the sofa, drawing her stocking feet up yoga-style and assuming either he would change the channel or they would now watch the after-game talking heads.

But Carter only turned off the TV and tossed the remote on the side table next to him. "Come here," he said, leaning back against the sofa arm and actually crooking a finger.

She stayed right where she was. "What? You think I'm Sally all of a sudden?"

He chortled. Apparently, he found her so very amusing. "You're always so cool, Paige. Lately, I've been thinking that your being cool is damn hot." He gave her a long, low-eyed look. She felt his gaze tracking, down over her red sweater and jeans, to the Christmas tree socks she'd put on to feel festive—and then right back up again until he once more met her eyes. "There's so much I never realized about you before, so much I want to do with you."

Speaking of hot, maybe she ought to turn off the fire…

"And *to* you," he added in that low, rough voice that made her want to do things to him, too. He lightly nudged her knee with his toe. "Come on over here so I can show you how much I like you."

She chewed on her lower lip for a moment, truly torn. She *wanted* to go there. She wanted it bad. "You're supposed to be giving me time, remember?"

He said a swearword under his breath—and then, lightning quick, he sat up, reached out and grabbed her arm. She smacked at him with her free hand.

That didn't stop him. He just held on and hauled her back with him, pulling her on top of him, stretching out with his head on the sofa arm and her all over him like a blanket.

She glared down into those gold-flecked green eyes. "This is not fair."

He lifted himself up, but only enough to catch her lower lip between his white teeth. She gasped at how disgustingly good it felt. He worried the tender flesh briefly and then let it go. "Where'd you ever get the idea it was going to be fair?"

Her lip tingled where he'd bitten it—not hard, oh, no. But sharply. Excitingly. Her hips were pressed to his, her breasts to his chest. It was like stretching out on a flesh-covered slab of rock—hot rock. All of him, chest, belly and lower down, all hot. And under the fly of his black jeans, things were not only hot, but getting harder, too.

Before she could remember that she needed to stop him, he eased a hand up under her hair to cradle the back of her head. And then, so gently, he guided her down until her lips settled over his.

She groaned—a groan of protest that somehow came out like a moan of pleasure instead. He smelled all showered and fresh, and he tasted of beer and the promise of great sex. And then there was all that rock-hard hotness going on.

His hands roamed her back, sliding down and cupping her bottom the way he'd done at the shop, cupping her and pulling her closer, making sure she could feel every inch of that hardness beneath the fly of his jeans.

She wanted to drag him up the stairs to her bedroom and have her way with him. Repeatedly.

But she was not going to do that. No way. She was *not*.

"Not, not, not," she moaned as she made herself pull her mouth free of his. She glared down at him and tried to come up with the right words to make him see how wrong it was for him to keep taking advantage of her like this.

But then he said, "So, then. I'm thinking tomorrow I'll take you to Denver to pick out the ring."

"What did you just say?" She gaped down at him. Since this afternoon, she'd been doing a whole lot of gaping.

"The ring, honey. We need to get you an engagement ring."

Honey? Oh, no way. With a cry of frustration, she scrambled off him, sliding her feet to the floor and bouncing to a standing position. Bracing her fists on her hips, she glared down at him. "May I remind you—*again*—that you're supposed to be giving me time to think over whether any good at all can come from this crazy idea of yours?"

He laced his hands behind his big fat head. "And I've decided that you've got it all wrong."

"Wrong?" She made a few sputtering sounds.

And he blithely continued. "Yeah. You're wrong. It's not time yet for you to think it over."

"Not *time*?" She raised both hands, palms to the ceiling, and then let them flop in complete frustration to her sides. "What are you even *talking* about?"

"Very simple. First, we have to get through our trial engagement, see how it goes, you know? And *then* is when the thinking part comes, meaning that's when we consider whether or not to actually get married."

"But I haven't even decided if I—"

He put up a hand. "Hold on a minute." He winced as he sat up, and then he cast a rueful glance at the obvious bulge in the front of his jeans. "Look what you did to me, Paige."

"What *I* did?"

He had the nerve to nod. "Sex is important, Paige. And we need to start having some. But you gotta agree that it wouldn't be a good example for Dawn, if I'm in your bed and we don't have any kind of formal commitment."

"Formal commitment?! It's a fake engagement you're talking about here."

He dared to look wounded. "It's not fake, no way. Just because we're testing the waters, that doesn't make it fake."

That did it. "I can't do this right now. You've got me so turned around, I can't think straight. You need to go."

Shaking his head, he reached for his boots and put

them on. She stepped back as he rose. Sally, by the fire, got up and followed him into the front hall, Paige trailing after.

He took his jacket from the peg and put it on, grabbed Sally's leash, then wrapped those long, strong fingers around the doorknob.

But then, instead of pulling it open, he reached for Paige again.

This time she was ready for him. "Oh, no, you don't." She jumped back before he could grab her.

"Let down your guard, Paige." Now his voice was rough and low. He coaxed, "Come on. Have a little faith. It's going to work. Just give it a chance and you'll see it's the right thing for both of us."

God, when he looked at her like that—eyes all hot and full of feeling, as though there was no other woman in the world but her…

It wasn't a good idea, this wild plan of his. But she really, really wanted to go with it anyway. She wanted to have sex with him. She wanted to *be* with him, desperately, be his woman, his fiancée—even if it only lasted till Christmas.

Which was most likely just what would happen. She'd be crying by Christmas, her life a complete mess.

She tried to make him admit that. "You're refusing to see the whole picture here. We work together, we're best friends. This idea of yours could ruin everything. It could completely destroy what we have."

"No way."

"Carter. Come on, think about it. *Really* think about it. What if it doesn't work out? What if…one of us falls in love and the other doesn't?" *What if one of us is al-*

ready in love? "What if it ends up destroying our friendship, our partnership, everything? Then what?"

He just wouldn't listen. "That's not going to happen."

"You can't be sure of that."

"Yes, I can. Nobody's falling in love. That's the beauty of it. We know who we are with each other. We're going to have a great life together, Paige, a *happy* life. That falling-in-love crap isn't going to happen to us."

But it's already happened to me.

And yes, she should simply tell him that. But she couldn't make herself do it. She knew what would happen if she did.

He'd be out the door in an instant. How sad was that? She was in love. And she wanted a chance with him. She couldn't stop thinking that this ridiculous test-drive engagement of his was the only way for her to get her chance.

Her chance to have everything—and also, her chance to lose it all. "I mean it, Carter. You have to give me some time. You have to let me think it over."

"How long?" he demanded. He clicked his tongue at Sally. She trotted over and he bent to clip on her leash.

"You've got to give me a week without pressuring me." Sally looked up at her as she spoke—and then turned to Carter when he said, "A week's too long. We need to move forward."

"Not until I have time to think about it."

"Two days." Carter glared at her as if he wanted to strangle her—strangle her or grab her and tear all her clothes off.

She glared right back at him. "I can't believe I'm bargaining with you about this."

"Two days." He growled the words. "And then we're on."

"Two days and then *I* decide."

"You always have to have it your way." His voice was hard. Cold.

Her heart ached. But she stood her ground. "Two days. Absolute minimum."

"Fine. Two days. And then you decide."

Chapter Six

The next morning when Paige went downstairs, there was no sign of Carter. No perfect pot of coffee brewing, no delicious bacon sizzling in the pan. Just Biscuit whining at the door to get out.

She walked Biscuit, made the coffee herself and fixed breakfast for her and her sister.

Dawn had questions. "How come Carter's not here? Is this about you and him? Is he having trouble dealing with your telling him how you really feel?"

Paige debated explaining everything. But no. Her baby sister didn't even need to hear it. And Paige certainly didn't feel like telling it.

She evaded Dawn's questions.

At work, Carter kept his promise. He was civil and distant. She hated it, the distance. Yes, he was only giving her what she'd asked for. She knew that. Still, she missed her best friend.

The next day, Tuesday, he was out of town trying to track down a car for another rebuild. His absence made things a little easier. She could almost pretend that everything was as it used to be. Except for the ache in her heart, which wasn't as it used to be at all.

That night, Paige was no closer to knowing what to say to him than she'd been when she asked him to give her some time. Tomorrow, she needed to give him an answer. Unfortunately, she didn't have one.

Thus, at two in the morning, she remained wide-awake, tossing and turning in her bed.

If she'd been asleep, she might not have heard the tap on the window. That probably would have been for the best.

But she did hear it. And instead of ignoring it, she shoved back the covers and went to investigate. Biscuit jumped down from the end of the bed and followed her over there. Slowly, she eased the blinds open.

The window overlooked the side yard. In the faint gleam of starlight and the soft spill of the streetlamp bleeding in from the curb near the front of the house, she saw that a light snow was falling. She also made out the shape of a man hunched on the slope of roof right beyond the glass.

Carter.

Of course.

His eyes gleamed through the slit in the blinds. "Let me in, Paige." The window muffled the words. Still, she heard him.

So did Biscuit. He whined in delight at the sound of Carter's voice and his tail got going like a metronome, slapping at the back of her calf.

Serve the man right if she just shut the blind all the way again and went back to bed.

But knowing Carter, he would only keep tapping, calling her name louder, until she gave up and let him in.

She yanked the blind up. The window opened to the side. She pressed the latch and pushed it wide. Cold air and the smell of a winter storm had her wrapping her arms around herself and shivering.

His white teeth flashed with his grin. "For a minute there, I was afraid you'd tell me to get lost."

The screen remained between them. "I'm still debating that," she muttered. "What are you doing on my roof?"

"Getting to you."

"Maybe you've forgotten." She ladled on the sarcasm. "I'm supposed to have till tomorrow to give you an answer."

"It *is* tomorrow," he announced way too loudly. "Get rid of the screen."

"Shh!" She cast a glance at her bedroom door, which was shut. But still. Noise tended to carry in the middle of the night. "Keep your voice down. You'll wake up Dawn."

"Sorry." He didn't sound one bit contrite, but at least he'd lowered his voice again. "The screen…?"

She gave in, grabbed the little tabs at the base and eased it out of the frame, pulling it into the room and propping it against the wall, then stepped aside to make way for him. He extended a long leg over the sill, turning his thick shoulders sideways so they would fit through the opening. For a moment, she dared to hope the window was too small for him. But with a little maneuvering, he was in. "Brrr," he said, turning to slide the window shut. "Brisk out there." He seemed to fill up the room with his big self and the cold, wet smell of the snow that clung to his shoulders and dusted his hair. Biscuit whined again. "Hey, buddy." Carter dropped to a crouch and started scratching his ears. "Turn on a light. It's dark in here."

She trudged to her tangled bed, dropped to the edge of the mattress and flipped on the lamp.

Carter rose again. She watched as he shrugged out of his heavy jacket and tossed it on a chair. "Biscuit. Lie down." He snapped his fingers and pointed at the doggy bed on the corner. The dog trotted right over there and flopped down, which totally annoyed her. She could never get that dog to go to his bed, but Carter made it happen on the first command.

"You look cute in those pajamas," he said. "What are those, dogs?"

"Dachshunds," she muttered glumly. "Dachshunds in Christmas sweaters and holiday beanies."

He came to her then and sat down beside her, bringing the tempting scents of winter and manliness and a faint hint of aftershave right along with him. "Cute." He fingered the soft flannel of her sleeve.

She pulled her arm free. "It hasn't been two whole days and you know it."

"I couldn't wait." He nudged her with his elbow. Gently. And then, low and hopefully, he asked, "So, what's the verdict?"

She stalled, like the big fat chicken she was. "Why couldn't you just come in the front door like a normal person?"

He frowned. "I don't know. It seemed kind of wrong to just let myself in at two in the morning. And I didn't want to ring the bell and wake Dawn up, get her all freaked out, wondering what's going on…"

"Right." She wanted to stall some more, get all up in his face for disturbing her in the middle of the night, insist that he could have waited for daylight, at least. But instead, she stared into his wonderful, beloved face and admitted the awful truth. "God, Carter. I missed you."

Which, of course, had him smiling that knee-melting smile. "You did?"

She gave it up completely. "Yeah. A lot. I missed you a lot." And then she hung her head and scowled down at her flannel-covered thighs.

"Hey," he said so softly, so coaxingly. And he caught her chin with a gentle finger and made her look at him. His eyes twinkled much too brightly and he teased, "Merry Christmas to me."

She made a snorting sound, but he didn't let that stop him. He just eased his other arm around her shoulders and drew her close to his side. She went without protest. After all, close to him was exactly where she longed to be. She lifted her chin for him when he guided it higher so he could claim her mouth.

A kiss ensued. A fabulous, wet, hot, very long kiss.

Still kissing her, he eased her back across the bed. She gave in to his urging, lifting her arms and wrapping them around him, kissing him some more.

However, when he started unbuttoning her pajama top, she caught his hand. "Stop." She opened her eyes and waited.

Eventually, he lifted himself away from her just enough to demand, "What now?"

She put on her sternest expression. "Carter. I mean it. You have to slow down…"

"Whatever you want." He sat up.

She sat up, too. Tugging her pajama top back into place, she made a halfhearted attempt to smooth her tangled hair.

When she looked at him again, he was holding out the most beautiful diamond ring she'd ever seen. Even in the dim light from the bedside lamp, the gorgeous thing really sparkled. "What in the…?" Words failed her. That happened a lot around him lately.

"Be my fiancée, Paige." He caught her hand and slipped it on. Perfect fit, wouldn't you know? The enormous oval diamond winked at her from the bead-set platinum band.

"My God, Carter." She held it toward the light and the big stone glittered madly. "This looks like the real thing." She glanced at him accusingly.

His fine mouth flattened out. "Of course it's the real thing."

"It must have cost a fortune. Did you ask them what kind of return policy they had?"

"Will you for once in your life not worry about the damn money?"

"Someone has to. You never do."

"Only the best for my fiancée." He slid over nice and close again and went back to work unbuttoning her jammies.

Paige looked down at his big hands as he slipped the first shiny red button free of the button hole—and just like that, it all came painfully clear to her.

She knew exactly what she had to do.

"Carter." She took off the ring, removed his hand from the second button of her pajama top and placed the beautiful diamond in the middle of his calloused palm.

"Damn it, Paige. What's your problem?" He shot her a hot, wounded glance. "It's a no? How can it be a no? I thought you said you missed me. I thought—"

She put a finger to his warm, beautiful lips. "Shh. It's not a no."

Twin lines formed between his eyebrows. "I don't get it."

Her heart trip-hammered against her ribs. "There's something I have to tell you before I can give you a yes."

A relieved sigh escaped him. "Fine. Go for it." He waved the diamond at her. "And then take this damn ring back so we can get on with the plan."

Slow, careful breaths, she reminded herself. It had to be said. He really needed to know. "Remember that silly magazine quiz you took for me the Monday before Thanksgiving, when we were waiting for Deacon Leery to see us?"

"What's that got to do with anything?"

"Bear with me. Do you remember?"

"Yeah. What about it?" He gazed at her blankly, waiting for the punch line.

She delivered it. "Well, Carter, you were right. You answered every one of those question just as I would have. And they were excellent questions, really. Which is why that was the day I realized I'm in love with you."

His eyes widened—and not in a good way. "You… *what*?"

She took another slow, deep breath and said it again. "I'm in love with you, Carter."

He shot off the bed, turned and backed toward the window. Shaking his head, he accused, "You're lying," in a low, furious whisper. "And that quiz? I was only messing with your head, only having a little fun, that's all."

Sadness weighed her down. Yeah, she'd known he hated it when women said the *L* word. Still, she'd kind of hoped he might react differently if the words came from her. So much for hope. Stifling a sigh, she rebuttoned her top button. "I know it was only a joke. To you."

"Uh-uh. No." He stuck the ring in his back pocket. "You're not in love with me, Paige. You're too smart for that crap. This is just your way of getting me to back off."

Was there ever a man as thickheaded as this one? "I'm not lying, Carter." She made herself look him straight in the eye. "I'm in love with you and if I did say yes to you, it would be because you, um, fill up my heart and make my world better. Because you're hot and I want you. A lot. Because I love to be with you and you make me laugh and I can always count on you. Because you make my coffee just the way like it. Because you're both a stand-in dad and a big brother to my baby sister." She tried a wobbly smile. He didn't return it. "But I *would* be dishonest to go into this, er, engagement plan with you if I didn't tell you upfront how I feel. So I'm telling you. I'm in love with—"

He threw up both hands. "Stop saying that." He scooped up his heavy jacket from the chair where he'd tossed it. "I…can't tell you that back. I'll never tell you that. I don't believe in that, you know I don't."

She did know. The guy just wasn't going to the love place. He'd always been perfectly clear on that.

And what did he think? That this "awful" revelation had been easy for her? It hurt to see that horrified, get-me-out-of-here look on his face. It hurt a lot.

Still, she'd done it. She'd told him the truth about the state of her heart. Now they could move on. "Well, all right, then. We can give up this crazy test-drive engagement plan and go back to the way it's always been."

"No," he argued, for no possible reason that she could see. "Did I say I wanted to call it off? I never said that."

"But, Carter—"

"No, Paige. I mean it."

"You mean what?"

"I just need a little time to deal with this information, okay?"

"Um, sure." Had she ever in her life had such a bizarre conversation? Not that she could recall. "Take all the time you need."

He shoved his arms in his jacket. "You know, you're acting really…sane about this, I have to say."

"Uh. Thanks."

"You're amazing, Paige. One of a kind."

"Wow. Great," she replied without much enthusiasm.

"I just need to think this over a little."

"No problem."

He turned and slid the window wide. A gust of wind and snow swirled in as he faced her again. "We'll talk."

"Sounds good." Paige wrapped her arms around herself against the sudden chill.

He actually attempted a smile. "Well, all right. Night, then."

"Night, Carter."

And he turned again, squeezed his big self out onto the roof and disappeared from sight.

Biscuit woke her before dawn. He stood at the bedroom door, whining to be let out. She crawled out of bed and opened the door. He left.

But not fifteen minutes later, he was back again, sitting at the side of the bed, his tail sweeping the rug, panting and staring up at her hopefully. She knew what that look meant. Carter had not come by to walk him.

"Fine," Paige grumbled. Biscuit wagged his tail harder. "I'm coming, I'm coming…" She shoved back the covers and got dressed.

Outside, beyond the front porch, a thin blanket of white covered the yard and the walk. Snow dusted the hedge tops and clung to the branches of the evergreens.

"Pretty, huh, baby?" she asked the dog. Biscuit whined and tugged the leash. "Heel," she said firmly.

For once, he obeyed, falling back to his place at her side. They went down the steps and out to the sidewalk. She walked him around the corner, down three blocks, and then back home, stopping to let him take care of business, her plastic bag at the ready.

The neighborhood looked so beautiful all covered in white. Most of her neighbors already had their lights and wreaths up, some had even left the lights on all night. So cheery and Christmassy. It really lifted her spirits.

She was smiling when she got back to the warm, cozy house. She went straight to the living room and turned on both the tree and the mantel lights.

Dawn came down as she was scooping coffee into the coffeemaker. "No sign of Carter, huh?"

Not since about two-thirty this morning. "Nope. Poached eggs?"

"Sure. Don't ever tell him I said so, Paige. But I miss him when he's not around."

"Your secret is safe with me."

Dawn went to the cupboards to get down the plates,

mugs and flatware. "Looks like we got about three inches of snow."

"Yeah. It's gorgeous out there."

Dawn carried the plates over to the breakfast nook. "So, are you two going to work out this, um, whatever it is that you're not explaining to me?"

"We definitely are," Paige replied with a lot more confidence than she felt. "Eventually."

At nine, when Paige walked into BCC, Carter was already busy in the shop. He hardly spoke to her that day. She returned the favor. Friday was pretty much the same.

By Friday evening, all the snow had melted. Paige drove home through the snow-free streets, telling herself that it was all for the best. She'd done the right thing, to lay all her cards on the table with Carter. In time, she would get over him. He would stop feeling he had to avoid her. They might have a nice, straight-ahead talk about how foolish they'd both been.

And then their relationship could go back to the way it used to be.

In the meantime, she would be fine. Tomorrow was her day off. She didn't even have to set eyes on the man. She would go to Rocky Mountain Christmas on Central Street and shop until she dropped.

That night, Dawn and Molly went to a party at a friend's house. Paige raided her DVD stash and found *Love Actually*, *While You Were Sleeping* and the Wynona Ryder version of *Little Women*. She watched them back to back, with a carton of Ben & Jerry's and a jumbo bag of peanut M&M's for company.

She told herself how great it was that Carter wasn't there. He would have insisted on watching *Bad Santa* or something equally gross, guy-centric and R-rated.

She didn't need him. Uh-uh. She and Ben & Jerry were doing just fine on their own.

Dawn came in at midnight. They watched the end of *Little Women* together. When they went upstairs, Dawn took Biscuit to her room. The dog was a total bed hog, so Paige could look forward to tossing and turning without him in the way. She washed her face and brushed her teeth and donned her other Christmas pajamas—green flannel with dancing elves. Ho-ho-ho and all that jazz.

The last few nights had been awful. She'd hardly slept at all, her mind on Carter and her hopeless love for him and the best friendship she missed so much. That night, she assumed, would be pretty much the same, probably with a little indigestion thrown in from all the ice cream and candy.

But she climbed into bed and turned off the lamp—and must have fallen asleep right away. The next thing she knew, she heard a sound at the window.

"Huh?" She gaped at the bedside clock. It was ten after two.

Tap-tap-tap. "Paige?" *Tap-tap.* "Come on, let me in…" *Tap-tap-tap...*

Paige popped to a sitting position. *Carter.* At the window.

Again?

She blinked away sleep and raked her hair out of her eyes and refused to get excited at the prospect of seeing him.

"Paige." More tapping. "Come *on…*"

"Fine." She turned on the lamp, pushed back the covers and took her time crossing the room. Drawing up the blind, she slid the window back.

"Hey." He gave her a happy grin.

"This has got to stop, Carter."

"Don't be cranky. I needed to see you."

"I was sound asleep."

"Sorry."

"You're out of control, you know that?"

Now he put on his pitiful face. "The screen. Please?"

She gave in and pulled it free of the frame. Once he was in, she folded her arms tightly across her middle and ordered, "Shut the window. It's cold out there."

He shoved it shut and shrugged out of his big jacket. "Don't be mad at me."

"What are you doing here?"

"We need to talk."

"*You* need to talk, apparently. And always in my bedroom in the middle of the night." And why did he have to look so totally manly in old jeans, older boots and a frayed BCC Grand Opening T-shirt from five years ago? It just wasn't fair.

He gave her the sexy eyes. "You look so cute."

"I look like I was sound asleep. Probably because I *was*."

He gave her a slow once-over. "I think I like the elves better than the wiener dogs."

She refused to soften toward him. "You've barely said a word to me since the last time you climbed in my window, and now suddenly you're all about my festive pajamas and how we *have* to talk? Uh-uh. You are not making me feel any more kindly toward you."

He looked at her sideways and asked in a voice both rough and way too tender, "But you still love me, right?"

She made a scoffing sound. "And you wonder why all your women turn into drama queens. You drive them to it."

"Be nice, Paige." He reached out and wrapped his big fingers around her upper arm.

Even through the fuzzy flannel of her sleeve, heat sparked and sizzled across the surface of her skin. She pulled her arm away. "Start talking."

"Can we maybe sit down?"

"Sure." Head high, she marched to the bed and dropped to the edge.

He eyed her warily for a moment, but then came and sat beside her, just as he had two nights before. A weird and awkward silence ensued—because no way was she starting the conversation when *he* was the one who just *had* to talk at two in the morning.

Finally, he opened with "So…you're okay, right?"

"Other than my annoyance with you for interrupting the first sound sleep I've had in days? Yeah. I'm fine." She flashed him a sharp glance. "And if your needing to talk consists of you asking me questions and *me* doing most of the actual talking… No, Carter. Or, as you would say, *Hell to the no*."

He grumbled, "So, then you're really pissed at me, huh?"

"And there you go with yet another question."

He shot her a glance both bewildered and contrite. Really, for a man who couldn't run away fast enough at the mere mention of the word *love*, he was altogether too lovable.

And then he glumly confessed, "I don't know how to start."

And she couldn't just leave him there, hanging, all on his own. She put her hand over his big, rough, hot one. When he turned it palm up, she laced their fingers together.

He gave her a sweet little squeeze. "As far as you being in love with me…?"

Her heart rate accelerated and her mouth went dry. "Yeah?"

"Really freaks me out."

"I noticed." She made herself look directly at him. His beautiful tawny eyes were waiting.

He lifted their joined hands and brushed those amazing lips across the backs of her knuckles that peeked out, just barely, between his big fingers. "But it's okay."

"What's okay?" Her breath had kind of snagged in her throat. She made a conscious effort to suck in air and let it back out slowly.

"I mean, if you can be in love with me and be okay with it, so can I."

Okay? He said it was *okay*?

That was…very, very *not* okay. "Carter, I have to tell you. When I get married—*if* I ever get married—I want the man I marry to be more than just 'okay' with me."

"But I *am* more than just okay with you."

She shook her head. "Sorry. Not feelin' it."

"But it's true. I'm gone on you."

A burst of laughter escaped her. "Oh, come on."

His eyes darkened and his jaw hardened. "Don't laugh at me, damn it. It's really…kind of a stunner for me, too, you know? I'm not sure what to make of how I feel about you now. But whatever this is, I do feel it. I've got a real thing for you. You're something special, Paige. Special and drama-free and wonderfully sane."

Sane. How romantic.

Not. "Carter, I just think…" Her sentence trailed off into oblivion.

Because he messed with her concentration by leaning closer and nuzzling her ear. "Plus, I gotta ask..."

A lovely shiver went through her. One she tried to make light of. "Oh, great. More questions."

"Don't get all judgey. This is a *good* question. I think you're going to like it."

"Of course you do."

He nibbled on her earlobe. And then he pulled his hand free of hers—but only in order to wrap his arm around her and tuck her in close to his side. He stroked her hair, pausing to free it from where it was all tangled up in the collar of her pajama top. His touch and his closeness felt so good, so right. And she kind of loved the way he touched her, fussed over her. So much so that she couldn't quite make herself push him away.

And then he leaned even closer. "The question is—" he nuzzled her temple and his warm breath teased her ear "—how'd you get so damn hot, Paige?"

She made the mistake of turning toward him. Now she looked directly into those molten green eyes. And had he always smelled this good—like pine trees and mountain air and a hint of high-grade motor oil?

He captured her mouth.

She moaned. She couldn't help it. His tongue pressed the seam where her lips met. And she gave in without even token resistance, gave in to him instantly, sighing in welcome.

Oh, that kiss. *His* kiss. She should have known better than to let him put that mouth of his on hers. His kiss weakened her everywhere—her shaking knees, her quivering belly, her yearning heart and definitely her mind.

He guided her back to the bed the way he'd done two nights ago, so she lay across the mattress, her bare feet dangling just above the rug. The whole way down he kept his lips locked to hers, kissing her about as close to senseless as she could possibly get without actually losing consciousness. She sighed some more and clutched his thick shoulders and fervently wished that she would never have to let go.

But then he lifted up enough to ask, "Well?"

Her eyes popped open and she stared at him blankly. "Um…" Her mouth tingled from that kiss of his. Oh, who was she kidding? Every inch of her tingled. "What was the question?"

"How come you're so hot?" He went to work on the little green buttons of her pajama top.

"I think it's your fault." It came out breathless with yearning. "You do it to me."

"Paige, sweetheart…" Oh, that voice of his, so deep and rough and wonderful. His voice touched her, stroking her, arousing her every bit as much as his big hands and his clever mouth did. He kissed the tip of her nose, and one button slipped free. He moved on to the next and the next after that. She didn't even pretend to try and stop him.

And what do you know?

In seconds, he had all those little green buttons completely undone.

Undone. Yeah. Exactly. He'd undone her buttons. He'd undone *her*.

She gazed up at him, dazed and way too willing, her hands still clasping the hard curves of his shoulders. He took them—one hand and then the other—and guided them back onto the mattress to either side of her head.

And then he got hold of her unbuttoned pajama top and peeled it wide. She felt the cool air of the shadowed bedroom on her bare breasts.

"So pretty," he whispered as he lowered his head. He sucked her nipple into his mouth.

Paige gasped and then she moaned. She tried to lift her hands again to hold him, pull him closer to her.

But he didn't let her. With a low chuckle, he caught both her wrists and pressed them into the mattress.

"Fine," she complained in a breathless little whisper. "Be that way."

He made a rough sound, a knowing sound. That sound vibrated against her willing flesh as he suckled her breast, flicking her aching nipple with his tongue, nipping it lightly with his strong teeth.

Surely this couldn't be happening, she and Carter in her bedroom in the middle of the night, doing the things people do when they're a lot more than friends. Surely this couldn't be real.

Oh, but it was.

He kissed her other breast. She shuddered in delight and lifted her body toward him. He let go of her wrists then—in order to undo the little satin bow at the top of her pajama bottoms. She lifted her head off the mattress and watched in heated awe as he eased them down and tossed them away.

"Carter, I—"

"Shh, Paige. It's okay…"

She blinked and stared down at herself. Naked. Except for her pajama top spread wide against the sheet, she was naked.

She was naked and Carter, still fully clothed, was sliding to his knees by the side of the bed. He guided her legs apart and moved in between them, taking her by the waist, pulling her closer to the edge of the bed, then easing her thighs up onto his shoulders. She let him do all that, let him position her just where he wanted her. She didn't make a peep of protest, gave him nothing but a willing sigh. She let him see all of her, and she felt not even a hint of reserve or shyness.

"Relax," he whispered.

She did relax. She let her head drop back to the bed as she felt his breath across her skin. Her body hummed with pleasure as he laid a burning trail of kisses up the inside of her right thigh.

And he didn't stop there. He pressed that clever mouth of his to the eager flesh stretched over her hipbones, brushed those lips in places she knew she shouldn't let him go.

Ah, but she did let him. She more than *let* him. She welcomed him, opened wide to him. She surrendered. To his hot kiss, to the heat that seemed to roll off his big, hard body in delicious waves.

To the magic in his hands.

Oh, he was good at this. So good that she cried out more than once and he had to reach up and press his fingers to her lips and whisper, "Shh. Shh, now, sweetheart..." before he went back to driving her crazy with his lips and his tongue and even his teeth.

And did she mention those hands?

Oh, my, those hands. It so wasn't fair what he did with those hands. He had her completely at his mercy.

And at his mercy, as it turned out, was a great place to be.

She felt her body rising, the tide of pleasure cresting. And she rode it joyfully, spreading her arms wide on the bed, clutching the pillows, the blankets, the sheets, grabbing tight and holding on, tossing her head, moaning his name, trying to keep from shouting out loud as her climax rolled through her.

In the middle of it, as she came apart completely, he rose and joined her on the bed again. He kissed her, taking her mouth as his fingers continued making magic down low. His lips were so warm. He tasted of her own arousal, and he kissed her so deeply as the waves of pleasure pulsed and shimmered all through her. She hit one peak, dared to think it was over…

But it wasn't over. She faded down a fraction, started to catch her breath—and it was happening all over again. The pleasure receded only to bloom hot and glorious once more.

When it finally ended, she just lay there, body limp, little sparks of giddy light flashing pleasantly on the insides of her eyelids.

"Paige?" He kissed her name onto her slack lips.

She sighed. "What now, Carter?"

"Say yes, Paige."

She opened her eyes and looked at him as he stared down so intently at her. His mouth was swollen, red from kissing her. She could feel his erection, hard and hot, against her side, pressing at her through the fly of his jeans. And his eyes were so green right then, green and deep. And way too determined.

All at once, she felt very naked. She fumbled for the sides of her pajama top to gather it around her.

He caught her hand. "Don't hide from me. Just say yes. Just say you'll be my fiancée, say we'll be together. *Really* together. Say I can stay with you, here, tonight, in this bed."

"Oh, I don't think that's a very good idea."

"Will you stop with the negatives? Show me the positive. Give me my yes."

"Carter…" She reached up then and touched the side of his face. "Tonight I ate a carton of ice cream, watched a bunch of girlie movies and told myself I was licking my wounds, moving on…"

He turned his mouth into her hand and kissed her palm. "Say yes, Paige."

She knew she should remind him again of all the ways his crazy plan would be flirting with disaster. But really, he was such a terrific man. He'd always been so good to her, generous, caring, there at her side whenever she needed him.

And now that she'd had a taste of him, well, she really didn't want to stop.

He said, "We can be good together, better than ever. I know we can. I just want my chance with you."

That got to her. After all, she wanted the same thing. *Her* chance with *him*.

Why *shouldn't* they try it? Why assume it would all go to hell in the end?

After all, it was the season of miracles. Maybe the miracle she wanted most of all would happen. She and Carter would work it out and end up making a life together, building a family, having it all.

He bent close and rubbed her nose with his. And he didn't stop there. He pressed soft, tender kisses on her cheek, along her jaw and then on her mouth.

Generous. Yes. He was a generous man. Even in bed.

And she couldn't hold out against him any longer, didn't *want* to hold out.

"Say yes." He breathed the words into her hair. "Have a little faith, Paige. Take a chance on me."

By then, she'd all but forgotten all her very good reasons for telling him no.

She just wanted what he wanted, the two of them, together. To be his through the holidays, to get her chance to show him that love didn't have to equal insanity.

"Yes, Carter," she whispered. "All right. I accept your proposal. We'll try your Christmas engagement and see how it goes."

Chapter Seven

Carter could hardly believe it. “You just said yes.” At last. It was happening. They were on. “Tell me I’m not dreaming.”

Paige gave him that beautiful, soft little smile of hers. “You’re wide-awake. And we’re in this.”

He kissed her, hard and quick. And then he sternly instructed, “Do not move.”

She laughed. “Carter, what—?”

“Stay right there.” He cut her off before she could get rolling. “Stay just as you are. Don’t move and don’t say a word.” She looked amazing with her clothes off, all soft and so touchable, with all that velvety pale skin, her dark hair wild against the white sheet, those fine breasts with their dusky nipples that fit his hands just right…

Paige Kettleman. Naked for him. Who knew?

And the way she’d come apart for him? That had been

something special. All signs were good they would share a smoking-hot sex life.

She pressed her sweet lips together and widened her eyes at him to let him know that, okay, she would be quiet and she wouldn't move. Maybe for thirty seconds—a minute, tops.

That should do it.

He got up, fast, and reached back to get hold of his T-shirt, whipping that puppy over his head and off in an instant. He jumped on one foot and then the other, pulling off his boots and getting rid of his socks. After that, there were only his jeans and his boxer briefs. He reached in a front pocket and pulled out the three condoms he'd brought because a man who knows what he wants needs to be prepared to get it.

A flick of his wrist and the condoms landed on the bedside table next to the lamp. Paige was still quiet, still all eyes. Other than the wide eyes and the pressed-together lips, she hadn't moved a muscle. That wouldn't last long.

He ripped his fly wide. Careful of his damn close-to-painful erection, he took both jeans and boxer briefs down in a single motion, stepping clear of them, giving them a kick toward the bedside chair.

Paige's eyes had gone wider than ever. And his minute of silence was up. "Carter..." She said his name on a soft exhalation. And then she slipped her arms out of her pajama top and held them out to him.

He couldn't get back to her fast enough, going down to the bed and gathering her into his hungry arms. She snuggled right in.

Damn, he did want her. He wanted her bad.

He tipped up her chin to take her mouth.

And wouldn't you know? Being Paige, she started talking again. "Wait. I need you to promise me…"

He groaned. "Did you happen to notice I'm about to explode here?" She laughed. And he grumbled, "Right. I suffer. You laugh."

She lifted her mouth and gave him a quick, sweet little kiss. "I just need your agreement on one thing."

He teased, "As if I could refuse you anything in this condition."

She snuggled in closer. She felt really good there, her head tucked in against his chest. "It's about Dawn."

"What about her?" He kissed the top of her head and then ran a hand down the silky skin of her outer arm.

She tipped up her chin then and he looked down into those coffee-brown eyes. "As long as we're test-driving our relationship, we're going to be discreet for Dawn's sake."

"Discreet…" Did anyone but Paige even use words like that?

She pinched up her mouth at him. "Yeah. Discreet. You've got to be out that window before daylight. And whenever we spend the night together, we have to work it out so she doesn't have to know."

"How's that going to happen? She's eighteen and not in any way an idiot."

"We're going to *make* it happen, somehow. I need your word on that, Carter."

He combed his fingers through her hair. It smelled like vanilla and flowers. He wanted to bury his face in it, rub it on his chest, wrap it around the part of him that was getting very impatient to continue what they'd started. "I don't like sneaking around."

"Says the man who keeps climbing in my window in the middle of the night."

He traced the indentation of her spine. Slowly. With pleasure. "You're not going to budge on this, are you?"

"Nope."

"All right. Have it your way. I'll be gone before daylight and we will be discreet."

She gave him a glowing smile. "I appreciate that."

He thought about the ring then. "I didn't bring the ring tonight. I started thinking that maybe I was pushing it, choosing it for you. That maybe you wanted to pick out your own ring."

"I *love* that ring." She said it fast, without taking time to think about it.

He knew she meant exactly what she said. "Well, good, then. You got it."

But then she started thinking. Paige *always* started thinking. "You know, maybe we should pick out something a little bit—"

"Don't you dare say 'cheaper.'" He gave her a lowering look meant to signify that she shouldn't poke the bear.

"Well, really, now, Carter, I don't need such an expensive—"

"Stop. You like it and I chose it for you. It's yours. Discussion over."

"I cannot believe that we're sitting here naked, arguing about an engagement ring."

"So stop arguing. Let's go back to the part about how we're naked and take it from there."

Her answer came softly, almost shyly, "Okay."

His mama had caused no end of trouble for her children, but she never raised a single fool. Carter swooped down and captured Paige's fine mouth, pushing his tongue right in, loving the taste of her as much as the feel of her in his arms.

As he kissed her, he scooted them both around so they could stretch out on the pillows. He kicked the blankets down all the way, trailing kisses over her soft, strong little chin and into the sweet-smelling curve of her throat where the skin was so delicate and tender. He couldn't resist sucking that softness against his teeth, knowing it would leave a mark, forgetting already that they were being *discreet*.

Paige wrapped her slim arms tight around him and pushed her beautiful breasts against his chest. She whispered his name urgently, encouraging him to kiss her some more.

He was just working his way downward over her delicate collarbones when all at once, she had him by the shoulders and she pushed herself up. She pressed him back against the mattress, dark eyes shining with intent to take the lead.

Hey. No problem. She drove him crazy with her bossy ways a lot of the time.

But in bed, he could be flexible. He liked to run things, yeah. He also enjoyed it when his woman stepped up and demanded a little control.

She looked down at him through lazy, shining eyes. "Oh, Carter. So many muscles. I might have to kiss them all."

He didn't object and she got right to work on that, scattering kisses across his chest, over his shoulders, along the side of his neck. And then down. She wrapped her soft hand around him. He gritted his teeth and tried not to embarrass himself.

And then she took him in her mouth. He closed his eyes and gave himself up to the pleasure she offered.

But it had been a while. After the disaster of Sherry, there'd been no one else. And Paige's mouth all over him, well, that brought him to the brink way too fast.

He reached out, fumbling for the nightstand. She glanced up and met his eyes as his fingers closed around one of the condoms.

Now, there was a great view. Paige with her soft mouth all around him, that silky hair falling to one side and tickling his thigh, those big, dark eyes so soft and sexy…

"Can't last," he confessed with regret.

And she reached up and took the condom from him, getting it out of the wrapper and down over his aching hardness in no time.

"Come up here." He took her by the shoulders. She let him pull her up so they were face-to-face. And then he kissed her. He really, really liked to kiss her, to spear his tongue in and taste her, so sweet and wet and open to him.

At his urging, she straddled him. He reached down between them to hold himself in place.

And then, so slowly, she lowered herself onto him.

Oh, yeah. That was something special, Paige taking him in. He sucked in air slowly, letting it out with care, keeping his eyes open so he could watch her move on him. He drank in every line, every curve, every sigh and sweet shudder as she took all he had.

When she was almost there, he couldn't resist. He caught her soft hips and yanked her down harder.

She let out a hot cry.

"Shh." He reached up, touched her mouth in tender warning. "Shh..."

She started to move then, staring straight in his eyes, her hair falling forward, her pretty breasts swaying, her hands braced at his chest. She started to move...

And then he was the one making noise, groaning so loud and deep she bent right down close and teased, "Shh," against his mouth.

That was right before she kissed him again, her clever tongue slipping between his parted lips, sweeping the inside of his mouth, driving him wild as she kept rising and falling above him, pushing him to the limit, taking him right to the edge.

He hovered there, just barely keeping himself from going over, determined to feel her go first.

But she went on kissing him, went on moving so perfectly, lifting and falling, driving him closer. He was losing the battle, and he knew it. He wouldn't be able to hold out.

So he wrapped his arms around her and rolled them.

On top, he had a chance to outlast her, to hold on to control long enough to feel her shatter around him—Paige, all around him.

For the very first time.

She gazed up at him, eyes hazy with need, a tiny knowing smile curving the sides of her mouth. He lowered his head and covered her mouth again, taking that smile for his own, rocking into her as she lifted her legs and wrapped them good and tight around his waist.

After that, sensations rolled over and through him so fast, he lost all control. Heat sizzled and burned along every nerve. He surged into her and she took him, rocking beneath him, holding him tightly, just as he held her. He felt the end coming.

And then, just before he lost himself inside her, she cried out, sweet and lost and beautiful. He still had his mouth on hers and he drank in that cry.

Her body tightened around him in the first wave of her climax. So good, so right. He pushed into her harder. And then he held it, held still within her as her body pulsed around him and she moaned into his mouth.

That did it. He lost it. He threw his head back and groaned at the ceiling as the finish plowed through him, mowing him down.

He got up long enough to deal with the condom and then he returned to gather her close. For a while, they just lay there, all wrapped up in each other, drifting. He stroked her back and she cuddled in close. Her breathing evened out.

She'd fallen asleep.

Worn out, poor baby. The past several days had been hard on her and he knew he was to blame for that.

Because she loved him. Because she knew the way he was, not going for the love thing, no way. Because she'd tried so hard to hold out against him and he wouldn't let her do that.

But things would be better now. They were together just the way he wanted it. He would take care of her and she would be fine.

Had he rushed her to bed?

Maybe a little.

But he'd felt driven to seal the deal with her. And he was glad that he had. He wanted this, with her. He wanted it a lot. Wanted it so much that he had to be careful not to overthink it. His mother had been right, though he would never admit that out loud. He distrusted strong emotions, especially when he felt them about a woman.

But then again, the woman in question here was Paige. Paige could keep a level head even when the *L* word was involved. She'd always amazed him, the cool she had at her command.

Except in bed. She really came apart in bed. Which was the one place he didn't care how touchy-feely and explosive things got.

Yeah. He just knew it would all work out fine.

One thing nagged at him, though.

With all the tension between them, they hadn't been talking much in the past several days. He'd yet to tell her that Willow had bought the property on Arrowhead Drive, that she'd offered it to him as a bribe, an incentive to get married.

He needed to let Paige in on that, ASAP.

But who knew how she'd react? She could get cold feet, start wondering if he only wanted to marry her for the deed to the property. He could lose the ground he'd finally gained.

Maybe he should hold off on telling her. Just for a little while. She'd said she wouldn't be checking in with the Realtor again until after the holidays, so he had some leeway. He could wait a few days before he brought it up.

Right now the top priority was showing her just exactly how good they would be together.

In his arms, she sighed and a cute little snoring sound escaped her. Grinning, he tucked the covers over her and then slid carefully from the bed so as not to disturb her. She had her own private bathroom, a good thing, or he'd have to take a chance on wandering the upper hall, maybe disturbing Dawn.

When he came back to Paige, she was still sound asleep. The clock by the bed showed five minutes of four. He knew he should leave.

But damn, she looked so sweet and peaceful. He wanted to wrap himself around her, snuggle in tight and close his eyes. Just for a little while. He could sleep with her for an hour, then get up and go, come back and get Biscuit, take him out with Sally for their morning walk.

Then he'd make breakfast for the three of them, just like always. All nice and discreet, the way Paige wanted it. Dawn would have no clue of where he'd spent the night…

Carter woke to morning light shining in the window he'd climbed through the night before.

Paige slept on, sprawled on her stomach, one slim, soft arm thrown across his chest, her head turned toward him. So tempting, her hair tangled across the pillow, lips softly parted, totally conked out. He wanted to turn her over and kiss her awake.

But no.

She wouldn't be happy if she found him in her bed when he'd promised to be long gone by now. He needed to get out of there before she realized he'd blown it.

It took a lifetime, easing out from under her arm and inching his way toward the edge of the mattress. He took a lot of care not to let any cool air get in under the blankets. At one point, she sighed and stirred. He froze with one foot on the rug and the other still on the bed, holding his breath, certain he was about to be busted.

But she only turned her head the other way and went on sleeping.

She didn't even move after that. He made it out of the bed and into his clothes. Shrugging his jacket on, he turned to the window and slowly, carefully, slid it wide.

Cold morning air flowed in. He worried that the change in temperature might wake her.

But she didn't stir. He hoisted himself over the sill and out to the roof. As quietly as possible, he eased the window shut. Crouched outside, his breath a white mist, he peered through the glass.

No movement from the bed. Excellent. But she'd be waking up any minute now. Time to get the hell out of there.

He considered leaving the way he'd come, going up the gable and dropping to the roof of the garage, crossing it and using that big tree in the far corner to climb down into the front yard.

But going out through the backyard would be safer. He could slip out the side gate and avoid the possibility of one of her neighbors coming out to grab the morning paper and spotting him wandering around on Paige's roof.

So he went the other way, staying low to avoid detection, moving quickly to the covered porch that ran along the back of the house. He scuttled down the porch roof to the edge of the shingles, which was only about ten feet from the ground.

He could make that jump, no problem. So he launched himself outward, staying clear of the guttering, neatly landing and rolling, coming up in a crouch.

At which point, from behind him, Biscuit started barking.

He whirled, rising, as the beagle zipped out the kitchen door that Dawn had just opened for him.

Busted.

"Hey." Carter gave Dawn a sheepish wave, then dropped to a crouch again to greet the panting dog.

Dawn, looking half-asleep in pajamas, a giant sweater and heavy socks, folded her arms across her middle and tipped her head to the side. "Carter, what's going on?" she asked on a yawn.

He scratched Biscuit's floppy ears. "Thought I'd drop in."

"From the roof?"

He tried for humor. "I considered the chimney…" When she just looked at him, he made it worse. "Ho-ho-ho?"

For that he got a hard sigh and a definite eye roll. "Where's Sally?"

"Sally?"

"Yeah, Carter. Skinny red dog? Lives at your house?"

"Right. Sally. Well, see, I, uh…" He cast about for a plausible lie. Nothing came to mind. And then Biscuit took off, sniffing his way toward the back fence. Carter still had nothing, so he offered, "How 'bout some coffee?"

Shaking her head, Dawn turned from the doorway. At least she left it open for him to follow her in.

Paige entered the kitchen to find Dawn sitting at the breakfast bar watching Carter make the coffee.

She knew instantly that things weren't quite right. The dogs were not sprawled on the floor as usual after their morning walk; Carter still wore the same jeans and T-shirt he'd worn when he climbed in her window five hours earlier; and Dawn was too quiet—she had a strange, thoughtful look on her face as she watched Carter spooning grounds into the filter.

Dawn glanced over and spotted Paige in the doorway. She squinted and frowned. "What's that on your neck?"

"Where?" She pressed her hand randomly to the left side of her throat.

"No, the other side..."

By then Carter had started the coffeemaker and turned around so Paige could see his face. The guilty look he wore said way more than Paige wanted to know. He cleared his throat nervously. "Ahem. It kind of looks like a bruise..."

"Oh. My. God." Dawn blinked as disbelief slowly turned to understanding.

Paige slapped a hand over the spot. She couldn't believe it. Damn Carter and that sexy mouth of his. She glared at him.

He muttered, "Sorry..."

And Dawn accused, "Down the chimney. Right." She swung her gaze to Paige again. "I just caught Carter jumping off the roof."

Paige sent her brand-new fiancé another dirty look. He'd not only given her a hickey; he'd failed to keep his promise and go home before daylight. "What am I going to do with you?"

Dawn was the one who answered. "Have sex with him, apparently." She snorted. "I just might be scarred for life, knowing that."

Paige went on glaring at Carter, who responded with "Come on, Paige. We need to tell her what's going on."

"Yeah," Dawn agreed. "The truth. Novel concept."

Paige left the doorway and went to sit on the stool

next to Dawn. When Dawn sent her a grumpy look, she wrapped an arm around her and pulled her close. "I wanted to be discreet for your sake."

"With Carter involved?" Dawn gave her a fond head butt. "Good luck."

"Hey," Carter groused. "I can do discreet."

Paige and Dawn made identical scoffing sounds. And then Paige said, "Carter's asked me to marry him…"

It was really pretty sweet the way Dawn's eyes lit up. "And…?"

Carter stood a little straighter. "She said yes."

Dawn threw both arms wide, almost whacking Paige across the face. "At last!" And then she grabbed Paige and hugged her. "Oh, I knew this would happen eventually. Finally! This is totally amazing. Not to mention wonderful, terrific and just about perfect."

Was it? Paige hugged Dawn back and slid a warning glance at Carter over her shoulder. He'd better not start in about how they were test-driving their relationship. Dawn didn't even need to hear that.

Either he took the hint or didn't want to get into that part of their arrangement any more than Paige did, because he only said proudly, "I am one lucky man."

Dawn let out a giddy squeal of laughter, flew off the stool, zipped around the end of the snack bar and headed straight for Carter. He opened his arms to take her in.

She hugged him as hard as she'd hugged Paige. "You're moving in here, right?"

He caught her face between his hands and dropped a kiss on her forehead. "That's the plan. Eventually."

She looked at him sideways. "Did you actually climb in my sister's bedroom window last night?"

He busted to it. "Yeah. I kinda did."

"Because you didn't want to freak me out, right?"

"Yeah, pretty much."

"From now on, just pick a door, will you?"

"Okay, sunshine. I can do that."

"Good."

He let her go. "So, what do you want for breakfast?"

"Pancakes?"

"You got 'em."

Dawn asked, "How long has Sally been at home alone?"

"Too long."

"We should go get her."

"I'll do it." Paige slid off the stool. She was still in her pajamas and robe, but she'd only be out of the car long enough to run up and down Carter's front walk.

She headed for the garage, grabbing her purse from the closet in the front hall on the way.

So much for total discretion around Dawn, she thought as she drove to Carter's house. But then, why sneak around, really? It wouldn't work with Dawn, anyway. She was too smart for that. And she'd taken the news of the engagement well.

Better than well. Dawn had been so happy for them.

How bad would it be for her if things didn't work out, if the cons outweighed the pros when Paige and Carter evaluated their "test drive"?

Oh, please. Dawn would be fine. She'd survived and thrived even after losing both her parents way too young. She could no doubt rise above her big sister screwing up with Carter.

And was this a screwup?

On the rational level, it certainly felt like it. A try-out engagement? Pretty much a big helping of ludicrous drizzled in crazy sauce.

But on that other level, the level that had to do with Paige's hungry heart and her yearning body, with all the parts of her that *felt*, the parts that wanted and needed and burned, the parts of her she'd been denying ever since Jim Kellogg cut out her heart and then walked all over it?

On that level, desire had the lead now. She'd let Carter in her bedroom window and taken him to her bed.

It was done. She had loved it. She wanted more.

And she wouldn't focus on the negative, she promised herself as she pulled up in front of Carter's house. She was in this now. She was Carter's bride-to-be.

If she ended up crying by New Year's, so be it. She was going to love every minute of being Carter Bravo's Christmas bride.

Chapter Eight

That day was the annual Justice Creek shopping bazaar known as Rocky Mountain Christmas. Then, in the evening, they were going to the Holiday Ball at the Haltersham Hotel. Carter decided to take the whole day off work and spend it with Paige. He called Mona to tell her he wasn't coming in, then he went home to shower and change.

He was back within the hour and he brought a suitcase. Paige came down the stairs to meet him wearing her favorite soft white sweater, skinny jeans, knee boots and a bright red scarf.

He held up the suitcase. "I thought I'd bring a few things over. You know, for any time I stay the night…"

Was he pushing things too fast?

Without a doubt.

Did she care in the least?

Heck, no. She was *glad.* She smirked, "Moving right in, huh?"

"Oh, you bet." He was looking at her mouth. Something flared in his eyes. He dropped the suitcase and reached for her, dragging her close and nuzzling her neck. "You smell amazing."

She went to mush, just at the feel of his hard arms wrapped around her.

Dawn and Molly were already over on Central Street enjoying Rocky Mountain Christmas, so Paige didn't pull back when his kiss turned hot and deep.

And wonderfully slow.

When he finally let go of her mouth, he asked, "Dawn?"

"Gone with Molly."

"Perfect." He grabbed the suitcase in one hand and her in the other and dragged her back up the stairs to her room, both dogs following behind.

In the bedroom, he ordered Sally and Biscuit to lie down by the window. They did, without him having to say it twice.

He turned to her. "Now, where were we?"

"Why don't you tell me?"

"How 'bout I show you, instead?"

And he did. He took off everything she'd just put on and they spent a very satisfying hour doing what came naturally.

Then she pulled on a robe and helped him put his stuff away. There were empty drawers in the bathroom and plenty of space in the walk-in closet, including an empty bureau that had once been her dad's. The unpacking accomplished, he took the dogs downstairs and she got ready all over again to go to Rocky Mountain Christmas.

When she went back downstairs, she followed the

close harmonies of the Puppini Sisters singing "Santa Baby" and found him sitting in the living room with the fire going, looking at the tree.

He rose when she entered the room. "There you are. Close your eyes."

What was he up to now? "Why?"

He chuckled. She did love the sound of his laughter. In some ways, he didn't have a clue. But in others, well, he was one of a kind in a very special way. "Come on, give me some trust, Paige. Work with me here."

"Oh, all right." She shut her eyes. He moved behind her and put both his hands over her closed eyelids. "What? You think I'll cheat and peek?"

"You just might. You're sneaky that way."

She laughed and tried to elbow him.

But he only dipped out of range—and kept those big hot hands of his covering her eyes. "Behave."

"Okay. I surrender. Do with me what you will."

"Now you're talkin'."

"Except not right here in the living room. Dawn may be open-minded, but that doesn't mean she needs to see us cavorting naked in the parlor."

"I can't believe you just said 'cavorting.' And 'parlor,' too."

"Cavorting can mean either leaping and dancing around excitedly or applying oneself enthusiastically to sexual or disreputable pursuits."

He grunted. "I may not have gotten past junior college, but I do know what cavorting means."

"Just so you also know, we're not doing any of that here in the living room." Right then she felt his lips on the back of her neck, and a delicious shiver skittered down her spine and bloomed sweet and hot in her belly. "Stop that."

He chuckled. The sound was so lovely, rich and low and rough. He advised, "Then stop talking and let me do this thing—or I'll be forced to carry you back upstairs where we can cavort in private."

The idea of going upstairs again held great appeal. But they couldn't spend *all* of their time in bed. "Do the *thing*, then. Whatever it is."

He still had his hands over her eyes. "Turn around slowly." She did. He stayed behind her, covering her eyes. "Stop." She obeyed. "Now move forward."

"Toward the tree?"

"Are you peeking?"

"Of course not. But it *is* my living room and I know you turned me around a hundred and eighty degrees and that would mean I'm now facing the tree."

He laughed again.

"Why is that funny?" she demanded.

"It's just…*you*, Paige. Always with the calm and reasonable deductions." She would have asked him what, exactly, he meant by that. But then he added, "And I mean that in the best possible way."

She decided to be mollified. "So, then. Move forward, you said…?"

"Yeah. Move forward toward the tree until I tell you to stop."

She started walking. He came right along with her, his hands over her eyes.

By her estimation, they were maybe a foot from the tree when he said, "Perfect. Stop." She stopped, the shin of her right leg just brushing the sharp tip of what she recognized by feel as a lower branch. "One step to the right."

She stepped. "That's too far. Take half a step back." She did. "Bingo." His hands dropped away. "Now open your eyes."

She opened them and found herself staring directly into the brightly lit and heavily ornamented branches of the tree. "Wow. My Christmas tree. Who would have guessed?"

He put his hands on her shoulders. She felt his warm breath in her ear. "You're not paying attention."

Of course she was paying attention. She was staring right where he'd told her to look…

And then she saw it—her beautiful engagement ring, on which she knew very well he'd spent altogether too much money. It hung from a branch a foot from her face, spinning and sparkling on a short length of red satin ribbon. "Oh!"

He pressed his cheek to hers. "Merry Christmas, sweetheart."

Sweetheart. It sounded really good coming out of his mouth. "Carter…" She turned her head and kissed him—a short, sweet one. And then she took the ribbon off the branch and eased the end from the loop that held it to the ring.

When she had it free, he took it from her, caught her left hand and slipped it on. "Looks good," he said, his voice just gruff enough to make happy tears scald the back of her throat.

She twined her arms around his neck and kissed him again, a slow one this time, tangling her tongue with his, sighing when he reached down and pulled her in good and close so she could feel how much he wanted her, even with no actual cavorting likely again for hours and hours.

When he lifted his head, he asked, "Rocky Mountain Christmas?"

"Oh, yes, please."

They shopped and then shopped some more—well, Paige shopped. Carter went with her into just about every festively decorated store. He carried her bags for her and didn't complain once.

They ran into lots of friends, two of his brothers and three of his sisters, all of whom congratulated them when Paige showed off her ring. At a little after two, they met up with Dawn and Molly, who both squealed in delight at the sight of the ring.

All four of them were hungry, so they went to Carter's half sister Clara's restaurant, the Library Café, where they ate club sandwiches with steak fries. Carter had a beer and Paige, Dawn and Molly all had cappuccinos because they were the perfect drink for a cold, clear almost-winter day.

Carter dropped Paige and the girls off at the house at a little before five. He wanted to check in at BCC and he hadn't thought to bring a suit over, so he would return to his house to get ready for the Holiday Ball. He left Sally with Paige.

Sally was a sweetie. She kept Biscuit company. The two of them would sniff every inch of the backyard together. Inside, they spent most of their time sprawled on the kitchen floor side by side, drooling on chew toys.

Paige and the girls got to work primping for the big night. They showered and did each other's hair and helped each other get that smoky-eye look just right. Molly and Dawn gave Paige a bad time about the bruise on her neck, but both assured her that, once she'd dabbed on concealer, you couldn't even see it. Paige pinned up her hair and wore a vintage '50s emerald-green taffeta creation. The dress was ankle-length, sleeveless, with a draped collar, a fitted top and a giant full skirt. She'd found it on Etsy and fell hard in love with it, one of those dresses Christina Hendricks might have worn to the office Christmas bash on *Mad Men*.

The girls had already gone off with their friends when Carter arrived. He looked fabulous in his dark suit and he whistled at her and made her spin around so he could admire her '50s splendor from all sides.

And then he took her in his arms and he kissed her.

She clung to him and he didn't seem to mind. "You look so handsome." She brushed her fingertips through the short, coarse hair at his temple. "And I feel so happy…"

"Merry Christmas to us." And he kissed her again.

Right then she believed with all her yearning heart that it was all going to work out for them, that their test-run Christmas engagement could lead only to a walk down the aisle and happily-ever-after.

All the lights were blazing at the white, red-roofed Haltersham Hotel. Twin rows of beautifully decorated trees lined the walk up to the famous front portico where the ghost of Olivia Haltersham was still said to wander sometimes late at night. The frail and unstable Olivia had been the pampered wife of steel magnate Thor Haltersham, who had built the hotel back at the turn of the twentieth century.

Carter passed the car keys to the valet and ushered Paige between the glowing trees and up the walk to the wide front steps. She gave her short black velvet cape to the coat-check girl. They followed the crowd up a series of pink marble steps, beneath a heavily carved mahogany arch and then down a wide hallway to the entry hall that led to the ballroom with its giant windows topped by elegant fanlights. Those windows offered breathtaking views of the mountains. Accented in gorgeous dark woodwork like the rest of the old hotel, the ballroom's burnished floor gleamed in the light of the original Tiffany stained-glass chandeliers.

It was a magical evening, Paige thought. She danced with Carter, both of them laughing and swaying to the beat, having a great time. And when the band played slow songs, she went into his arms, her taffeta skirt rustling softly against the dark wool of his trousers.

He whispered such lovely things in her ear. He said she was beautiful and he'd always liked dancing with her—never more so than now, when he knew he would get to go home with her and stay the whole night.

Whenever they took a break, they were instantly surrounded by friends and family. Paige didn't mind at all being hugged and congratulated by Carter's siblings and half siblings. More than one friend said how they'd always known the two of them would end up together. Carter grinned and complained that he'd had to use all his powers of persuasion to get Paige to give him a yes. Paige laughed and said she'd tried her best to resist him.

Carter said, "In the end, I convinced her to give me a chance." He pulled her in closer, brushed a kiss at her temple and Paige couldn't help thinking that the evening had turned out just about perfect.

But perfection never lasts forever.

At a little after midnight, Paige and Carter were standing near the ballroom's gorgeous old rosewood bar, chatting with Carter's youngest sister, Nell. Carter had just told a silly joke. The three of them were laughing—and, then, in the space of an instant, Carter's face went blank and his eyes went flat.

Paige frowned up at him. "Carter, what…?" She let the question die unfinished because by then she'd spotted the problem.

Sherry.

Carter's ex, in a tight red velvet dress that showed off her lush curves, came right for them. She had her blond hair piled up high, tumbling in little curls along the graceful column of her neck.

Carter caught Paige's arm and pulled her behind him. He did it so fast, Paige didn't think to protest. Sherry kept coming, her wide red lips a grim slash and her eyes sparking fire.

The outspoken Nell remarked, "Oh, come on. Seriously?"

Carter sent his sister a quelling look as Sherry stopped short in front of him. He took a crack at civility. "Hi, Sherry. Merry Christmas."

But his ex wasn't having it. Sherry tossed her golden head. "You don't have to look at me like that, Carter. You don't have to put Paige behind you like that. I'm not going to *do* anything."

Paige wasn't sure she believed her. The blonde was a human explosion just begging to happen. Still, it felt more and more wrong to hide behind Carter, to peer over his shoulder as if he were her shield in case the bullets started to fly.

So she stepped out into the open and took his arm.

"Paige," he warned darkly. But at least he didn't try to drag her behind him again.

She aimed a smile at Sherry and said the first mundane thing that popped into her head. "Beautiful party, don't you think?"

Sherry never once took her gaze off Carter. "I only want to say that I hope..." She seemed to lose her train of thought. Her eyes had started glittering, filling with tears. One got away from her and trailed down her cheek.

Paige slid a glance at Carter. He looked miserable. Paige knew he saw the big scene coming. He hated big scenes and he had no idea how to keep this one from happening.

Paige tried, "Listen, Sherry. This is neither the time nor the place to—"

"Please." Sherry sniffed. She tipped her chin toward the art glass chandeliers overhead and announced furiously, "I hope you'll be happy, Carter. Very, very happy. Congratulations to you both. Long life and...a big family and everything you ever wanted."

Carter said carefully, "Thank you."

Sherry turned to go. Paige dared to hope that the worst was over—until Sherry threw her head back and let out a wild cry. Then she buried her face in her hands and started sobbing.

That was when Murray Preble materialized out of the crowd. "Sherry, I'm here," Murray said, his voice low and gruff, his eyes hot with passion. "I'll always be here."

Sherry sobbed all the louder and started walking—straight into Murray's open arms. "Oh, Murray," she cried. "It's happened, just like I always knew it would. He's with Paige now. Hold me, Murray. Help me. Please..."

Murray cradled her close and whispered something in her ear. Then he gazed over her golden head straight at Carter and gave Carter a slow, solemn nod. Carter didn't nod back. He stared at nothing, his eyes a million miles away.

Tenderly, Murray tucked a thick blond curl behind Sherry's ear. "Come on, now, honeycup, it'll be all right. Just give it time and you're gonna be fine." He turned her and ushered her toward the exit. She clung to him, staggering in her high heels like a crash victim reeling away from a horrible accident, until they disappeared through the open doors.

As if on cue, the music started up again.

Nell groaned, "Honeycup? Did he just call her honeycup?"

Carter muttered, "Murray's a good guy."

"Yeah. But...*honeycup*?"

"Looks like it worked for her. She went with him, didn't she?" Carter took Paige's hand. "Let's dance."

She hung back, worried about him. "Are you all right?"

"Yeah." He didn't really seem all right. His tawny eyes were distant. "Dance with me."

What else was there to do but let him lead her onto the floor?

They danced a couple of fast ones and then the band started playing a Christmas ballad. He pulled her close and wrapped both arms around her. They swayed to the music.

Eventually, he asked, "You okay?"

She pressed her lips to the side of his throat and breathed in the scent of his aftershave. "I am. I'm having a wonderful time."

He nuzzled her ear. "I hate big scenes."

"I know," she whispered. "Look at it this way. It's over and she's gone. There'll be no more drama tonight."

* * *

Half an hour later, Paige left Carter chatting with one of their customers from Boulder. The ladies' room in the entry hall had a line out the door, so she went looking for a better option.

The clerk at the front desk sent her down a hallway that branched off the lobby on the opposite side from the one that led back to the ballroom. It was a narrow hallway, and rather dim. The milk-glass wall sconces gave only muted light and the carpet was thick underfoot, muffling sound. The sign for the restrooms glowed greenish way down at the far end. And the holiday music from the ballroom? It seemed to be coming from some other dimension.

It really was kind of spooky. Paige shivered a little and a nervous giggle escaped her. People often claimed that the Haltersham was haunted. She might run into frail Olivia's ghost. Or the ghost of that woman who'd jumped from an upper floor back in the forties when she learned that her fiancé had died on the beach at Normandy…

She'd almost reached the green glow of the Ladies' Room sign when a woman's voice behind her said, "Paige. Wait a moment. I've been hoping for a word with you." Soft, cool fingers closed around her arm.

Paige stifled a thoroughly ridiculous shriek and froze in midstep. Turning her head slowly, not sure what to expect, she found herself staring into the ice-blue eyes of Carter's mom, Willow.

"Willow!" She eased her arm free and pressed her hand to her racing heart. "You surprised me."

"I'm sorry." A charming smile lit up Willow's face. "I really didn't mean to startle you."

What was she doing here? She hadn't been in the ballroom—had she? If she had, wouldn't she have said hello, at least? And Willow had always avoided town events. No one had mentioned she was coming tonight.

"I had no idea you were here," Paige blurted. "We didn't see you in the ballroom," she added unnecessarily.

But she never knew what to say to Willow. Carter's mom made Paige nervous. Who knew what went on in Willow's mind? She always seemed a little antisocial, somehow, as though she didn't really like other people all that much. She stayed in the mansion her husband had built for his first wife. And when she wasn't at the mansion, she traveled the world.

Willow laughed her sexy, husky laugh. She wore a clingy, calf-length black dress, low-cut, with spaghetti straps, and she looked absolutely stunning in it. "I only wanted you to know how happy I am for you and Carter. My son's a lucky man and I know you two are going to be as wonderful together as you've always been—only more so, of course, now that you'll be *truly* together in the fullest way."

Well, that was nice. Wasn't it? "Thank you, Willow. We're…very happy."

"I'm so glad." She caught Paige's arm again. Paige resisted the impulse to jerk free. "And please say that you'll let me give you an engagement party."

What? Willow never gave parties. Did she? "I, um…"

"I really want to do this, Paige. Say that you'll let me. We'll do it now, during the holidays. So romantic, to be engaged at this beautiful time of year. A dinner party, at my house, two weeks from tonight. I'll take care of everything. I promise to make it special. All you have to do is say yes and give me a guest list. I'll see to the rest. It can be as large or as intimate as you'd like it to be. What do you say?"

Who are you and what have you done with the real Willow Bravo? "Well, that's so…kind of you."

"Good. It's settled, then. Two weeks from tonight."

"Ahem. Well, we should talk it over with Carter, don't you think? If you'll just hold on for a quick minute while I duck into the ladies' room, we can go talk with him about it now."

Willow waved a hand. The huge diamond Frank Bravo had given her when he finally married her sparkled aggressively even in the gloomy hallway light. "Oh, I've already spoken with Carter. He's totally on board."

"Um. He is? He never mentioned a party to me…" And if she didn't get into that restroom soon, she was going to embarrass herself. "Just…" She held up a finger. "One minute. Promise. I'll be right out and we can go find Carter."

Willow gave her another radiant smile and a tiny nod. Paige took that for agreement and darted beneath the glowing green sign, shoving the door wide and rushing through.

All the stalls were empty. She ducked into the first one, slammed the door shut and eased her aching bladder just in time. Once that was taken care of, she washed her hands and hurried back out to rejoin Carter's mom.

The dim hallway was deserted. "Willow?"

No answer. Willow had vanished as mysteriously as she'd appeared.

Chapter Nine

"You're serious?" Carter didn't get it. And he really didn't like it. "My mother was here, at the hotel, tonight?"

"Yes. Just now. In a hallway off the lobby. She stopped me on my way to the ladies' room."

"I thought she was in Palm Springs..."

Paige shrugged. "Well, if she was, she's not anymore."

Dread tightened his stomach. Was this about the property? Had his mother told Paige about her insane marriage-incentive plan?

That would not be good. *He* needed to be the one to tell Paige about that.

Soon.

"Come with me." He took her hand and led her out of the ballroom and over to one of the long sofas that lined the walls of the entry hall. They sat down. "Now, tell me what happened."

"It was weird. She popped up out of nowhere. She said

how happy she was for us and that she wants to give us a dinner party at the mansion to celebrate our engagement. She wants to do that two weeks from tonight. She said that you're already 'on board.'"

"What else did she say?"

"What do you mean, what else?"

"Who knows?" he lied. "With my mother, you never do. So, that's all she said, then?"

"That's all—and *are* you on board for a party at the mansion?"

"How could I be on board? I haven't seen her or talked to her since…" About then, he realized he'd never told Paige that he'd had a drink with his mother on Thanksgiving Day. If he mentioned it now, Paige would wonder why he hadn't said anything about it before. She'd want to know why Willow would have asked him to come visit her alone that day.

He wasn't ready to go there. He just wasn't.

Paige prompted, "You haven't seen her since when?"

"A while. It's been a while." That sounded lame. He waited bleakly for Paige to demand when, exactly, *a while* might have been.

But she let it go. She fiddled with her necklace of emerald-green stones and chewed on her plump lower lip. "Don't be offended, but your mother's so…strange, Carter."

"Tell me about it." He hooked his arm around her shoulders and pulled her close. She leaned into him with a sweet little sigh. "Don't let it bother you, okay? Just forget all about it. I'll deal with her."

Paige pulled back and scrunched up her face at him. "Wait a minute. What does that mean, forget all about it?"

"It means you don't have to worry. I'll get us out of it."

"Carter, no. I never said I wanted to get out of it."

"Well, *I* want to get out of it."

"Why?"

"Come on. A dinner party at the Bravo Mansion?"

"What's wrong with the mansion? It's a beautiful house and I'm sure a party there will be lovely."

"Paige, it was Sondra Bravo's house and my mom stole it from her, just like she stole Sondra's husband. I don't like it there and I don't want our engagement party there."

"You're just being pigheaded."

"No, I'm not. You said it yourself. My mother is strange. We don't want to go trusting her with our party."

"But I think it was really sweet of her to offer and we need to..." Her voice trailed off as something sad happened in her big eyes. "Wait a minute..."

He didn't want her looking sad. "What? What's wrong?"

"This is about the test drive, isn't it?"

Crap. "No."

"Yeah." Now her pretty mouth was all pinchy. She leaned closer, but only to accuse in a tense little whisper, "I get it. You don't want your mom to go to all the trouble of putting on a party for us when we still don't know where we're going with this yet."

"That's not it at all." He said it a little louder than he should have.

She darted a glance around the hall and nudged him with her shoulder. "Keep your voice down."

"Sorry." He leaned in and spoke softly. "Paige. It's not about the test drive. My mother just... I don't trust her, okay? I know she must be up to something."

"Something like what?"

"How would I know?" Well, all right. He knew more than he was telling. And he needed to get honest with Paige.

Soon.

She said, "I don't know what your mother does when she travels, but here at home, she's kind of a recluse."

"So?"

There was eye rolling, followed by scoffing. "God. Clueless much?"

"My mother is my mother. It's not my fault."

"But if a situation arises where you can help her get outside herself a little, don't you think you ought to go with it?"

"Outside herself. What does that even mean?"

"You're being purposely thick."

Yeah, well. So what if he was? "You're saying that her giving us a party is going to help her, somehow?"

"I think it might. I think she feels ostracized by her past. I think she feels that people don't like her much."

He grunted. "Now, why in hell would she feel that way?"

"Carter. Be nice."

"Face it. People *don't* like her. She stole another woman's husband. She had five kids with him while he was still married to the woman she stole him from. And now she lives in that woman's house."

"It's *her* house now and the rest of that is way in the past."

"But it *happened*."

"And now it's over, and I've talked to your sisters and brothers."

"When?"

"Over the years—and don't look so suspicious. I'm

only saying what you already know. Your brothers and sisters want to put the past behind them. And your mother throwing our engagement party is a good way to help make that happen. Plus, I personally want to establish a good relationship with Willow. Saying yes to the party could be a nice start on that."

"Nobody has a good relationship with my mother. She's doesn't get close. It's not how she is." He spoke firmly, hoping she'd finally accept that he didn't want to do this.

Didn't work. "Well, I want to try. I agree that she and I will probably never be BFFs. But she's offered to do something nice for us, and I don't want to turn her down."

He knew that look in those fine eyes. It was the look she gave him when he insisted on paying more than he should for a car—multiplied by about a thousand. She was digging in her heels here and she wouldn't let it go until she had it her way.

She was way too damn determined about some things.

And apparently, his mother throwing their engagement party was one of those things.

Carter decided to look on the bright side. If he said yes to the party, that didn't automatically mean his mother would blab to Paige about the property before he found the right moment to tell her himself. If Willow intended to bring up the property to Paige, she probably would have done it tonight.

Right?

As if he knew. When it came to his mother, who could ever say?

He gave it up. "All right. I'll call her tomorrow and tell her we're going for it."

Paige's mouth lost the pinchy look. She leaned closer. "Thank you." She smiled full out and her husky tone spoke of good things to come. "We have to give her a guest list."

Damn. All those years they'd just been just friends. What a waste. They needed to have a lot of sex to make up for all they'd missed. "How 'bout we put the list together in the morning, before I call her?"

"Perfect." She brushed her lips across his and pulled away much too soon.

He ached to gather her close again and claim another kiss. But if he did that, he'd never want to stop. "You want to dance some more?"

She tugged on his collar, brushed a soft fingertip down the side of his throat. His mind wandered to more interesting places than the entry hall to the ballroom at the Haltersham Hotel. He wondered what she had on underneath that pretty green dress and how long it would be until he got to find out.

Then she leaned close again. "I was kind of thinking it would be nice to go home…"

He leaned in even closer—close enough to nuzzle her silky hair. "Let's get the hell out of here."

In Paige's bedroom, he ordered the dogs to sleep on the floor. They trotted over to the rug not far from the door and flopped down with a matched pair of gusty sighs.

"How do you get them to do that?" Paige was fumbling with her necklace.

He moved behind her and undid the clasp. "Just call me the dog whisperer."

She snickered. "Right." And then she held out her hand. He put the necklace in it. "Unzip me?"

He took her zipper down and peeled the sides of the dress wide. "Red lace." He ran a finger along the back strap of her bra. "I was wondering what you had under here."

She sent him a teasing smile over her shoulder. "I'm all about the holidays. Green dress. Red satin and lace." She peeled the dress down to her waist. He admired the slim shape of her shoulders, the sleek curves of her back. She shimmied the dress the rest of the way down, taking her lacy, frothy slip with it. Then, stepping out of both, she scooped them up in her free hand.

"What time does Dawn get home?" he asked as he watched her walk away from him, looking way too damn good in those high heels, the red bra and that itty-bitty pair of lace-trimmed red satin panties.

"Dawn's staying over at Molly's." She disappeared through the bathroom door, no doubt headed for the walk-in closet on the other side.

He just stood there for a moment, staring after her, thinking how great it would be to see Paige in her underwear every night for the rest of their lives.

And even better to get it off her. Possibly with his teeth.

Then he remembered he had way too many clothes on. He got busy, tossing his jacket over a chair, taking off his tie and his shirt. Stripped to the waist, he sat on the edge of the bed and whipped off his shoes and socks.

Paige reappeared without the dress, the slip or the necklace. And now her feet were bare.

He rose, undid his belt, slid it from the loops and hung

it over the headboard. "So if Dawn's at Molly's, I guess tonight we can be as loud as we want to be."

She wrapped her arms around herself, which pushed her breasts together over the lacy tops of the red bra. Burying his face there? Definite priority. "You *are* kind of noisy," she said, completely Paige-like, all smug and pulled together, even in nothing but her Christmas underwear.

"*I'm* noisy? Last night, I thought you would scream the house down."

She smiled so sweetly. "You kept shushing me."

"For Dawn's sake. But tonight, I might just let you scream."

She laughed. "As long as it doesn't freak out the dogs."

He dropped trou and then threw them at the chair. "Come here."

"Bossy, bossy." But she came to him. "Can I help you with those boxer briefs?" She didn't wait for his go-ahead, but got right to it, slipping a finger under the elastic waistband, sliding it back and forth against his belly.

The only word that came to mind was "Please."

She peeled off his boxers, going down with them, very slowly, to her knees.

When she got there she tipped her head and glanced up at him. Those eyes of hers, they saw too much. He sifted his fingers through her silky hair, smoothing the dark strands on her shoulders.

And then she wrapped her hand around him. It felt so fine it hurt. A low growl escaped him as she took him in her mouth.

Oh, that was something. Paige all around him, using her hand and that sweet, wet, hot mouth of hers, her silky hair brushing his thighs.

He let that go on for as long as he could bear it, and then he took her arms and lifted her, pulling her close against him, covering her mouth with his, kissing her endlessly as he removed her bra and got rid of those pretty panties. They still stood by the bed and that was fine with him. He kissed her breasts, let his hand trail down to the wet center of her.

She moved against his fingers, moaning, crying out. He never once shushed her. He liked when she made noise, loved when she lost herself, gave herself up to him, shattering from just his touch, once.

And then a second time.

After that, she pulled open the bedside drawer. He helped her, getting the wrapper off the condom, rolling it down over himself.

Then he turned her around and bent her over the bed. She went down, sighing his name. He pushed into her softness from behind, bending over her slim body so he could slide his arm around her and touch her while he moved inside her. He played her slick wetness with his fingers, rocking into her with long, slow, deep strokes until he felt her climax yet again.

That time, she not only cried his name; she said she loved him. She said it loud. "Love you, Carter. Love you way too much…"

No, he didn't believe in that crap. But still, he ate it up. It sounded damn good, now that it was coming from Paige. He'd never thought he'd ever get to be with her like this, get to see her come apart for him, and then make her do it all over again.

He moved faster. She rocked in rhythm with him. It felt so good. Exactly right.

The finish rolled through him. He bent even closer,

his body curling over hers. She reached back and wrapped her hand around his neck, turning her head to offer her lips.

He kissed her as he came, groaning hard into her open mouth. She tasted every bit as good as she felt.

In the morning, he got up without waking her and took the dogs out for a walk. When he returned, he found her at the kitchen table in her robe and elf pajamas, her laptop open in front of her.

The dogs went for their water bowls. He came up behind her, bent close and nibbled her neck. "What's up?"

She reached back and pressed her fingers over his fly. "You. As usual…"

He blew in her ear. "If you mock me, I won't make you breakfast."

She leaned back and he kissed her upside down. Then she explained, "I'm putting together the guest list for our engagement dinner. I figure I can just email it to your mother, right?"

Damn. He'd almost succeeded in forgetting that he had to call his mother that morning. "That'll work."

"You have an email address for her?"

"I don't remember it offhand, but yeah. I'll get it for you." He kissed her once more before rising and going to the counter to start the coffee.

He made them omelets with cream cheese, chives and Canadian bacon. Afterward, he tried to tempt her back to bed.

But she said, "Uh-uh. You need to call your mom. Do it now."

"Bad idea. She won't answer—or if she does, she'll be pissed off."

"Because?"

"She never gets up until ten." It was just nine. "Come on." He grabbed her hand and pulled her out of her chair. "This won't take long. I promise. I'll be on the phone to her at ten sharp."

Paige hung back a little, but the soft, willing curve of her mouth told him it was only because she loved to give him a bad time. He kissed her. She gave right in and kissed him back, after which he coaxed her up the stairs and out of her pajamas. Nothing like getting Paige naked to put the right spin on the day.

And he was as good as his word. They were back in the kitchen, fully dressed, at five after ten.

He called his mother.

"Carter, darling. How nice to hear your voice." He heard her yawn. "I'm so glad you called because I've been longing to congratulate you. I know you and Paige will be blissfully happy."

So far, so good. She hadn't mentioned the property. "Thanks, Ma. I'm a lucky man."

"Did Paige tell you I want to give you a party?"

He glanced at Paige, who sat next to him at the table, laptop open, still working on the guest list. "That's why I'm calling. To tell you that Paige thinks a party at your house sounds great."

"Only Paige? What about you?"

He couldn't resist a jab. "Well, I was already on board. Right?" Paige shot him a sharp look for that remark.

But Willow only chuckled. "You certainly are."

He gritted his teeth. "So, thank you and we accept." Now Paige beamed up at him.

"Wonderful," said his mother in her best tea-on-the-veranda voice. She named the date and added, "Seven for cocktails, with dinner at eight?"

He repeated the information to Paige, who nodded agreement. "Sounds good, Ma. We're on."

"I'm so glad. I asked Paige for a guest list..."

"She's getting it together right now. We'll email it to you today, if that's all right?"

"Perfection, darling." She gave him an email address. Paige passed him a sticky notepad and a pen. He jotted down the address and his mother said, "I'm leaving for Cancún tomorrow." Of course she was. "But Estrella will take care of everything, anyway. I'm just the hostess. I'll be home the day before."

"Great," he said, and felt more relieved than he should have that Willow was leaving again and reducing the likelihood that Paige would find out about the property before he'd explained to her that yes, his mother had tried to blackmail him into getting married, but that had nothing to do with why he'd proposed their Christmas engagement. "Have a good time."

"I will, darling. I always do."

"Thank you, Willow!" Paige piped up, loud enough that his mother heard it through the phone.

"Tell her it's my pleasure."

"I will, Ma."

"You should thank me, too."

"I thought I already did."

"Not for the party, darling..."

His gut clenched when she said that.

She laughed again. "I knew you would choose Paige. You just needed that nudge we discussed at Thanksgiving."

Matricide. Illegal. He had to remember that. "Bye, Ma. Safe trip." He hung up fast.

Paige was watching him. "You okay? You look a little pissed off." Her expression was tender and definitely sympathetic.

Maybe right now would be the best time to come clean, explain everything and reassure her that what was happening between them had zero to do with the property.

But then, what if she didn't believe him? He'd only just managed to convince her to give their engagement a go.

Uh-uh. He needed more time with her before he went into all that.

Paige raised a hand and waved it in front of his face. "Carter? You in there?"

He caught her wrist and pulled her out of the chair. "Right here." He hauled her close and wrapped his arms around her. "God, you feel good." He gave her fine bottom a two-handed squeeze.

"You are insatiable."

"Insatiable." He bent down and bit her neck. "I like that word."

"I need to get the guest list finished," she groused.

"In a minute. Right now you need to kiss me." He tried to capture her mouth.

But she got her hand up between them and pressed her fingers to his lips. Tenderly, she instructed, "Let me go..."

"Kiss me first. Help me forget that my mother drives me crazy."

"One kiss is not going to solve all your issues with your mother."

"Stop talking about my mother."

"You're the one who—"

He didn't let her finish. Pushing her fingers to the side, he captured that sweet mouth of hers.

By the time he let her go back to her laptop, he felt a whole lot better about everything.

Wednesday, Carter took Paige to a tree-decorating party out at the Bar-N Ranch, where his cousin, Rory, lived with her fiancé, Walker McKellan.

Most of the family was there—his sisters and brothers, and his half siblings, too. Some brought dates. Clara came with her husband, Dalton. Quinn brought his wife, Chloe. There was lots of food and plenty to drink and Christmas tunes playing nonstop. They all worked together to get the ranch house decked out right for the holiday season.

With everybody pitching in, the work went fast. The day before, Walker and Rory had cut down a beauty of a tree and set it up in a stand in front of the great room window. In record time, they had the lights strung and the decorations hung. Then they stood around the fire, shooting the breeze.

Nell was the first to mention the engagement dinner. "Guess what I got in the mail today?" She sipped a Black Russian.

Clara said, "An invitation to Paige and Carter's engagement dinner at the mansion?"

"You guessed it."

*Me, too*s filled the room.

Carter glanced at Paige. Her eyes were waiting. She mouthed, "That was fast."

Elise, his other half sister, said, "Those invitations

are gorgeous. Estrella's an artist, I swear. I mean, you could frame mine, I'm not kidding." For the benefit of friends not in the know, she explained, "Estrella's the housekeeper. She's a great cook, a brilliant organizer *and* she does calligraphy."

Clara said, "I'm so glad about this. This is big. Willow never does stuff like this. I keep asking her to come to family things. She always says she'll be out of town." She nodded at Rory. "Rory asked her to come tonight."

Paige was still tucking shiny ornaments into the mantel display. She arranged a gold pinecone just so among the pine boughs and said, "She's off to Cancún. Right, Carter?" At his grunt of agreement, she went on. "The dinner party was totally Willow's idea. She caught me at the Holiday Ball and said she'd like to give us a party."

"Wait a minute." Ice cubes rattled as Nell swirled her drink. "Mom was at the ball?"

Quinn and Chloe exchanged a doubtful look. Quinn said, "We didn't see her."

Garrett, Carter's other full brother, shrugged. "I didn't, either."

So Paige went ahead and told them about Willow catching her in the deserted hallway. "She looked beautiful," Paige said, "in a low-cut black silk jersey dress. I swear she doesn't look a day over forty—if that."

Jody, Carter's other full sister, who owned a florist shop on Central Street and was two years older than Nell, asked, "Did anyone but Paige see her that night?" There was a lot of head-shaking and a chorus of nos.

Paige said, "I know. It was strange. When she first grabbed my arm, I thought maybe I was about to come face-to-face with one of the Haltersham's famous ghosts."

"Weird," remarked Nell. "Mom is just weird."

Nobody disagreed. Carter could have added that their mother was also diabolical and manipulative and sometimes he wanted to strangle her. But he kept that opinion to himself and headed for the kitchen to grab another beer.

Quinn followed him in there. "Get me one, too?"

Carter took two longnecks from the fridge. "I think I need a little fresh air."

Quinn accepted the beer Carter handed him. "Mind some company?"

"Why not?"

They tossed their empties in the recycle bin Rory had set out in plain sight and went through the dining room to the front hall, where Garrett, beer in hand, joined them. Carter led the way out to the front porch, his brothers behind him.

Garrett hooked a leg on the porch rail. Carter and Quinn took the matched pair of carved wooden chairs that Walker, a skilled carpenter, had made himself. It was pretty cold, but they all wore thick sweaters, jeans and boots against the chill.

Carter glanced from Quinn to Garrett, thinking how they all three looked kind of like their father—big and bulked up. Quinn was a couple of inches shorter than Carter, his brown hair a shade lighter. Garrett, a year younger than Carter, ran Bravo Construction with Nell. He had almost-black hair and was the tallest of the three of them at six-four.

"I'm happy for you," said Quinn, tipping his longneck in Carter's direction. Carter tapped the bottle with his and they drank. Quinn nodded. "Paige is a winner and you two have always had something good going on."

"You lucky dog." Garrett knocked back a long sip. "All the good ones are getting snapped up."

Carter and Quinn snorted in unison. It wasn't as if Garrett was falling all over himself trying to find someone to settle down with. He liked the single life.

Garrett braced his shoulder against the porch post and nudged Carter's leg with his boot. "Mom giving a family party? Never saw that coming."

Carter took another long pull off his beer. "Paige wanted it, wanted to help her get 'outside herself.' Paige's words, not mine."

Garrett and Quinn exchanged freighted glances and Garrett said, "Yeah. We get that there's no way you were driving it." Of the three of them, Carter had always been the most impatient with Willow. He openly admitted his resentment of the choices she'd made and the childhood she'd put them through. Back in the day, he and his brothers and sisters had been known as the Bastard Bravos. It was a small town. Everybody knew way too much about everybody else. People looked down on them because their mom wouldn't stop having kids with another woman's husband.

Quinn, who had fists of steel and a heart of mush, said, "Be patient with Mom, bro."

"I'm trying. It ain't easy." He considered how much he was willing to say, and then asked Garrett, "She been after you to settle down?"

Garrett looked mildly terrified. "Hell, no. Why? She been after you?"

"Yeah. She kind of was. It's all Quinn's fault."

His youngest brother made a thoughtful sound. "Because of me and Chloe?"

"That's right."

Quinn settled deeper into the chair. "Marrying Chloe is the best thing I ever did."

Garrett challenged, "What about your little girl?"

"That goes without sayin'. Annabelle. Chloe. I got it all. Never thought I'd be this happy."

"And I'm happy *for* you," Garrett said. "For both of you. But just leave me out of it. I like being single."

Carter couldn't resist ribbing him. "You watch. Ma'll be after you next."

Quinn frowned. "Wait a minute. I'm getting the feeling she did more to push you toward the altar than you're telling us…"

Cater knew he'd already said too much. Still, he was kind of tempted to go all in, to tell his brothers exactly what their mother had done, and to ask them what they thought about his waiting for the right moment to go into it with Paige.

But why? It wouldn't matter what advice they gave him. He was going to do it his way, pick his own time—the *right* time—to tell Paige everything.

No call to go dragging Quinn and Garrett into it.

So he only shrugged. "Ma just got on me is all. She got after me to find a wife and start a family."

"And look." Garrett chortled. "It worked."

Carter had a sudden burning need to punch his middle brother in the face. But he settled for giving him the evil eye. "Don't even think that. Ma has got nothing to do with me marrying Paige."

Garrett put up both hands. "Don't shoot, big brother. I take it all back."

"Smart move." Carter drained the rest of his beer and stood. "We should go back in and join the party."

Quinn looked up at him, worry in his blue-green eyes. "You sure you're okay?"

"I'm good." And he was. He had Paige. She was not only his best friend now, she was *his* in the best kind of way. He liked sleeping with her, being able to stay at her house pretty much all the time. He liked *really* being a family with her and Dawn. And the sex with Paige? He loved that. Damn, if he'd only known. He wouldn't have wasted so many years just being her friend.

But Paige was all his now.

And he wasn't going to lose her, no way. They'd get through the test drive and end up together. He'd find a way to explain to her why he hadn't told her about Willow's skeevy trick sooner. It would all work out just right.

He had nothing to worry about. Not a damn thing.

Chapter Ten

That Saturday, Carter took another day off from BCC and drove Dawn to Denver to Christmas shop. Over the years, the trip had become an annual deal for the two of them. They left early in the morning.

Paige had a few things to go over at the shop, so she went in at eight. She made herself a cup of coffee and started running the numbers again for their expansion plans. It all looked good. She was almost tempted to give the Realtor a call, have her go ahead and make another offer on the Arrowhead Drive property. They could afford to pay more than they'd offered before Thanksgiving.

But first, she really ought to touch base with Carter. Not that he would care. He would go along with whatever she decided. Carter was the car genius. She was responsible for making the numbers add up. If she said she wanted to offer more and do it now, he would just say she should go for it.

Still, it was only right to run it by him before she made another move.

It had started to snow, pretty white flakes drifting by the window to the parking lot, when Mona came in at nine. Paige had the door to her office open and Mona stuck her head in. "What are you doing here on a Saturday?"

Paige got up and grabbed her mug. "Number crunching. Carter won't be in. He took Dawn Christmas shopping in Denver."

"I know." Mona headed for the K-Cup machine and Paige followed. "He sent me a text. It's not a problem. Jake and Billy can handle whatever comes up." The two mechanics were already at work out in the shop.

Paige and Mona chatted about Christmas shopping and the weather as Mona brewed herself a mug of caramel vanilla crème.

"White Christmas coming right up." Mona raised her full mug toward the window where the snow was coming down. Paige popped in a pod for herself and pushed the brew button. Mona asked, "So. How's engaged life treating you?"

"It's good." And it was. Overall. It did kind of bug her that she kept saying she loved him—mostly in bed when she kind of couldn't help herself—and he kept *not* saying it back. She shouldn't let it get to her. She knew how he was.

And her coffee was ready. She pulled the full mug out from under the spout. "Are you and Dean coming to our party at Willow's next Saturday?" Dean was Mona's husband of twenty-odd years.

"Wouldn't miss it." Mona sipped her coffee. "Carter's a good guy."

"I know."

"You two are great together."

"Thanks."

"So smile and act happy about it," Mona teased.

Paige laughed. "I'll have you know I *am* happy."

Mona nodded. "Excellent. To you and Carter and a lifetime of happiness." She raised her mug and Paige tapped it with hers.

In Denver, Carter took Dawn to Cherry Creek Mall and Larimer Square. They each bought gifts for Paige. Dawn helped him choose presents for his brothers and sisters. She shopped for Molly and Molly's mom. And they bought each other presents, too. It was part of their yearly tradition. They gave each other painfully specific hints about what they wanted.

Hints like, "Hey, Carter," as Dawn gestured grandly over a minifridge in the Macy's Home Store.

Carter scowled back broadly. "What do you need with a minifridge?"

"It's *convenient* to have a few fresh snacks in my room," Dawn replied, playing it adorably perky. "Plus, college? It'll be a freshman at CU before you know it. I'm so gonna need this in my dorm room."

"Forget it. I'm not dragging a minifridge all the way home." Total lie. He was definitely dragging that minifridge all the way home.

Once they'd clearly telegraphed what they wanted from each other, they both sneaked around, ordering each other to go elsewhere in the store so they could each grab the thing the other wasn't supposed to know about—even though they both knew damn well what the "secret" things were, because they'd each told the other exactly what they wanted.

Yeah, it was silly.

It was also great fun, teasing Dawn, the two of them running around the stores like a couple of fools.

Getting the minifridge under the camper shell in the back of his dually without her seeing him do it? A tougher job than most years.

But he made it happen.

Once they both got all their Christmas shopping handled, Carter always took her for a late lunch at the Capital Grille.

They'd just been served the Grille's signature cheeseburgers with Parmesan truffle fries, when Dawn announced right out of the blue, "You know, if you hurt my sister, I might have to kill you."

He set down the truffle fry he'd been just about to pop into his mouth. "Whoa, Dawn. Where'd that come from? I thought you were happy for me and Paige."

"I *am* happy for you. Mostly."

"Mostly? What the hell, Dawn?"

She sipped her Cherry Coke. "I love you, Carter. Everybody does. But you know how you are."

"Huh?"

"You heard me. I worry about how you are."

He picked up another fry, dredged it in ketchup and ate it before daring to ask her what in the hell she was talking about. "Okay. I'll bite. How am I, exactly?"

She cut her burger in half. Slowly. "You're a great friend. You're totally there for Paige—and for me, too. As a friend. But you're pretty old to be suddenly deciding you want to marry my sister."

He tried to make light of it. "Old? I'm not *that* old."

"Yeah, you kind of are. I mean, come on. There are statistics about guys like you. When guys your age who have never been in a long-term, committed relationship finally *do* get married, the chances of it lasting are not good."

He wanted to tell her that was a bunch of crap. But hadn't his mother said essentially the same thing? And that was kind of spooky, the more he thought about it.

Which made him decide *not* to think about it.

Dawn demanded, "What changed your mind all of a sudden?"

"Nothing changed my mind. I just realized that Paige is the one for me, okay?" Did he sound defensive? He wasn't. Uh-uh. Not in the least. He got to work on his burger, guzzled some beer.

Dawn took a few bites, too. Then she jabbed a fry in his direction. "You should take advantage of this moment and make me feel a whole lot better."

"Yeah? How?"

"Tell me how in love you are with my sister."

Love. Right. She just *had* to go and bring up love. "Look, Dawn—"

"See that?" She wiggled the fry at him. "That right there? You're scared to say it. And that's not good."

"You don't know what you're talking about." He said that in his firmest, most mature tone.

But Dawn was not impressed by his firmness and maturity. "I know exactly what I'm talkin' about." She sat back in her chair and gave him a tight little smile. "And *you* know how to convince me I'm wrong, but you are not doing it."

He threw up both hands. "Okay. Now I'm lost."

"Oh, no, you're not. You know exactly what you're *not* saying." She was too damn smart by half.

"Your sister's everything to me. I just don't believe in all that hearts-and-flowers crap, okay?"

"No, Carter. It's not okay. You've got a love phobia and you need to get over it. A man needs to be able to tell the woman he loves *that* he loves her. Paige deserves that. You know she does."

"You're way overcomplicating this thing."

"No, I am not."

"Plus, there is no such thing as a love phobia."

"Oh, yeah, there is. You have an irrational fear of falling in love."

He tried a little scoffing. "You're eighteen years old. What do you know about my supposed irrational fears?"

"Being eighteen doesn't make me totally oblivious. Unlike *some* people I could mention."

"Now I'm oblivious?" That kind of hurt.

Dawn tipped her head to the side and studied him for several long, uncomfortable seconds. "Look. I told you already, you're a great guy. But you've had a lot of girlfriends and none of them have lasted all that long. I just worry, I do. I don't want my sister hurt. Especially not by her best friend in the whole world."

"But I don't want to hurt her, Dawn. I would never hurt Paige. I want to *marry* her, make a family with her."

She had her hands in her lap now, and she stared down at them, hard. "My sister is the best there is."

"You think I don't know that?"

"She's only been in love once before in her life." Dawn spoke more softly now. She still refused to look at him. "And you know what that low-down rat did to her, dumping her flat because of me…" The tightness in her voice spoke of tears about to fall.

"Dawnie. Hey. Come on, now. Look at me."

"Fine." Dawn jerked her head up and glared at him through tear-shiny eyes. She dashed away the moisture with the back of her hand.

He had a clean handkerchief and he passed it to her. She yanked it from his fingers and dabbed her eyes some more.

He reminded her, "That guy wasn't good enough for Paige."

"I know that." She sniffed.

"And it's not your fault that Paige came home when you lost your parents."

"Of course it was my fault. She had to come home and raise me or I would've gone to my dad's sister, Aunt Mary Frances, in DC. Aunt Mary Frances never got married and works for the State Department. She keeps plastic covers on the furniture and is allergic to pets. No way could Paige do that to me. So she came home for me. She had no choice."

He couldn't let that stand. "It was *not* your fault, no way, no how. And Paige did have a choice. There's always a choice. Your sister made the right one—to take care of you, to keep your family together. And because she made the right choice, she got to see who that Kellogg creep really was before she went and married him."

Dawn wiped at her eyes again. "Well, I guess you're right about that."

"Yes, I am. And I'm not going to hurt Paige."

She gave him her best tough-girl scowl. "You better not."

"I promise I won't."

"Good. Because you'll *really* be in trouble with me if you do."

"Point taken. Eat your burger."

She grabbed it off her plate and took a giant bite, chewing aggressively and swallowing hard.

He suggested mildly, "Please don't choke yourself."

She reached for her Cherry Coke, sucked down about half of it and set the glass back on the table with purpose. "I do love you, Carter. I'll probably always love you, no matter what you do. And so will Paige. But you really need *not* to screw this up, okay?"

"I won't screw it up," he promised, and thought about the property. His mother would be back from Mexico in six days and Paige needed to know everything by then. "You can count on me," he added strongly, because he *was* going to tell Paige before Friday. He would get totally straight with her, lay everything out. "I mean that."

"Great." Dawn tried a wobbly little smile and then ate more of the burger, chewing more slowly this time. He went to work on his food, too. Eventually, she offered in her best peacemaking voice, "Share the hazelnut cake for dessert?"

He grinned wide, relieved and grateful that she wasn't staying mad at him. "What's lunch at the Grille without hazelnut cake?"

By the time they got in the pickup for the ride back to Justice Creek, Dawn's usual sunny spirits had returned in full force. She cranked up the radio and sang along to the holiday tunes while he griped that if he heard "White Christmas" one more time he just might lose his mind. It had been snowing on and off all day. Halfway home, the snow started coming down again.

They reached Justice Creek at a few minutes of four.

The dogs greeted them at the door. No sign of Paige yet. She'd said she was going to BCC that day and probably wouldn't be home until five or six. He helped Dawn haul all her loot up to her room. She gave him a hug and then went to Molly's.

Carter drove over to his place. He transferred the minifridge from the back of the pickup to the floor of his garage, dropped off his bags full of Christmas stuff, grabbed a change of clothes and returned to Paige's, where he took the dogs out for a walk in the snow.

When he got back to the house, the outside lights were on. So was the tree in the living room window. Paige must be home. He walked faster, eager to get to her, impatient with having to pause on the front porch to knock the snow off his boots.

He was just reaching for the door when she pulled it open.

God, she looked good. The light behind her brought out the shine to her dark hair, and those brown eyes were bigger than ever. Her fine mouth curved up in a smile just for him. How was it that the house always seemed warmer and brighter when Paige was in it?

"It's freezing out there. Get in here." She grabbed him by his heavy jacket and pulled him over the threshold. The dogs whined in greeting and danced around them as she shoved the door shut, turned the lock and engaged the chain.

Then came the best part. She melted into his arms.

The woman could kiss. How could he have lasted all those years without ever once having her tongue in his mouth? He loved the taste of her, the feel of her body under his hands, pressing against him. The smell of her—vanilla and coffee, something a little spicy, just so damn good.

He was hard in an instant.

She laughed. "It's nice how glad you are to see me."

"And to *feel* you..." He buried his face against her neck, scraping his teeth there, then licking the spot, too. She moaned.

And the dogs kept whining. Biscuit went up on his hind legs, pleading for Paige's attention.

Sorry, buddy. Me first. He lifted his head long enough to tell them both firmly, "Down. Go." Biscuit dropped to all fours again. With one more whine each, both dogs turned away. Their paws tapped the floor as they trotted to the kitchen and a happy reunion with their water and food bowls.

She asked, "Good day shopping?"

"The best. And that's saying something, given that I'm a guy and guys hate shopping."

"Dawn called. She said she had a great time, too. And she's spending the night at Molly's."

He bit her neck again and then whispered against her soft skin, "Good. Tonight I can see you naked in front of the fire."

"Where you're going to see me naked always seems to be a priority for you."

The stairs were right behind him. He shrugged out of his jacket and tossed it over the newel post. "That's because I've got my priorities in order." She wore a soft blue sweater dress, belted, with black tights and tall boots. He went to work on the belt, getting it undone and off her in seconds flat.

She slapped at his wrist. "Handsy much?"

He gave her his best wounded look. "I can't help myself."

"Yeah, right."

"Because there are so many places I want to see you naked and so very few hours in a day..."

She laughed as he undressed her, lifting her arms so he could whip off the big sweater, turning obediently to let him unhook her lacy pink bra. He got a little distracted from his purpose when he started kissing her breasts. She wrapped her hand around his head and held him close and whispered his name while he bit her nipple—gently—and flicked it with his tongue.

Eventually, he realized he had yet to reach the main goal. "Sit here." He took her by the shoulders and guided her down to sit on the stair so he could pull off those tall, sexy boots. Then he took her hand and stood her up and got to work on the tights. When she stepped out of them, he hung them on the newel post over his jacket.

That left only her little pink panties. She took them down for him and tossed them over her shoulder. "Ta-da!"

He bent and grabbed her around the waist, lifting her in a fireman's carry and heading for the living room as she laughed, kicked those long, silky legs and pounded his back with her fists.

When he set her down in front of the fire, she went right to work helping him get naked, too. He took the condom from his pocket and set it within reach as they stretched out on the rug together.

It was so good, better even than he'd imagined it might be, lying with her in the glow of the fire, snow falling outside. He kissed her, top to toe, and then he buried himself in her. She wrapped her arms and legs around him, holding him close to her, whispering his name.

At the end, she said the *L* word. “Love you. Oh, Carter, love you so much…”

He didn't say it back to her. He couldn't, somehow. Even though he knew what he felt. Knew what he had with her. Knew without any doubt that she was the one for him.

And had been for a lot longer than he'd ever let himself admit.

He lifted himself up on his arms and stared down at her, rocking into her, loving the way her pale skin flushed burning pink.

“Love you…” She opened her eyes then, and she looked right at him. “Love you,” she whispered, still contracting around him. She closed her eyes, turned her head to the side.

“Don't…” He bent closer then. But she kept her face turned away from him. So he caught her chin and made her turn to him. He covered her mouth and kissed her until she opened for him.

That did it, somehow. Her tongue came out and tangled with his and that tipped him over. He surged into her, kissing her so hard and deep as his climax shuddered through him.

It was all so romantic, Paige thought. Perfect really. Paige and Carter, all cozy, on a snowy winter's night.

But in spite of all that perfection, she wanted to cry. She really hated that she was starting to understand exactly, up close and personal, why all his girlfriends turned into drama queens eventually.

He was the greatest guy in the world—helpful, tender, smart. Funny, sexy, attentive.

But he just wouldn't let a woman get too close. And

that was beyond frustrating. It made her want to yell at him and start throwing things.

Carter whipped up some pasta with marinara sauce for dinner. Paige had brought home a fresh loaf of sourdough. She cut up a salad.

They ate in the breakfast nook, sharing a bottle of red, with candles on the table and the snow drifting down outside. The food was delicious.

And she was with the man she loved.

Perfect.

Except for that little problem he had with the word *love*. Except for how all of it was only a test drive with a plus-and-minus review waiting at New Year's.

Yep. She really got it now. Why all his girlfriends ended up throwing tantrums and calling him names. She felt more sympathy for them than ever lately. She thought of them fondly, wished them all well.

And she reminded herself that she'd gone into this knowing exactly what was up with him. She really did love him. And even if it didn't work out in the end, she was not going to regret this time they had together.

She was going to enjoy it, put her hurt feelings away and focus on the good stuff.

Because there was plenty of good stuff.

After dinner, they lingered at the table over second glasses of wine.

"I gave the books a good going-over at BCC today," she said. "We are so in the black."

"And that makes you happy." He gave her a relaxed smile. "I love it when you're happy."

"Good. Because I *am* happy." *About BCC's success, anyway.* "And I'm thinking maybe we should go forward with the Arrowhead Drive property. I can tell Kelly to up our offer, see if we can seal the deal before Christmas, after all. That way we can probably make the move by the end of January."

He had the strangest look suddenly. Vague and wary, both at once—and maybe just a little…what? Guilty? She was about to ask him what was going on when the look vanished and she wondered if she'd seen it at all. He drank some wine and settled back in his chair. "I don't know. What's the big hurry? Why not just wait like we planned? I don't want to pay more than it's worth."

She laughed. "You're kidding, right? You never worry about the money."

"Well, I just think our plan to wait till after New Year's is a solid one, that's all."

Good thing she'd checked with him before making a move. "It's always possible someone will come along and scoop it up while we're waiting for the owner to get reasonable about the price. You're okay with that?"

He looked out the dark bay window, where the snow was starting to pile up on the sill. "Paige, the property's been sitting there with no action for over a year. It's not going anywhere. And it's only a few weeks till the New Year."

"You didn't answer my question."

He stood, rounded the table and got behind her.

She tipped her head back to look up at him. "What are you up to now?"

Those gorgeous moss-green eyes held hers. He smiled a slow upside-down smile. And then he put his big hands on her shoulders, bent close and whispered in her ear, "Forget the property for now. It's all going to work out, you'll see…" He tucked a sweet kiss right there, behind her ear.

Her blood got thicker, her body felt warmer. Intelligent thought deserted her. "If you say so…"

"Um." He nibbled his way down the side of her throat. "Let's go upstairs."

"Why? You've already seen me naked up there."

"Exactly. And that's how I know it's something I really need to see again…"

Yeah, all right. Carter felt like a first-class douche canoe for not busting to the truth about the property when Paige had given him the perfect opportunity to tell all.

He could so easily have said, *We've already got the property. My mother bought it for us as a wedding present*. He *should* have said it, and then gone on to explain the whole truth.

But that was the problem: the whole truth didn't look so good.

What if she didn't believe him when he said the property had nothing to do with their sudden engagement? And already, he'd waited too long to tell her. That alone would make her wonder…

He decided not to think about it. Not right now.

He still had a week to figure out what to do.

Instead of getting honest, he took her upstairs and straight to bed, where he unwrapped her like a present—the best present ever. She was the gift that kept on giving. Every day, every hour, every minute he had with her only made him more and more certain she was exactly the woman for him, right for him in every way. Paige was totally no drama, the sanest woman on the planet.

Also, the sexiest in the most down-to-earth, *real* way. And funny and smart. He never got bored just hanging around with her. And now that she was his, he was never doing anything that might make her go away.

Sunday, they spent the whole day together, doing pretty much nothing. They walked the dogs, hung out with Dawn and Molly. They wrapped Christmas presents and piled them high under the tree. He stayed the night, same as he had every night since he'd finally gotten his ring on her finger. Daily, he moved more and more of his stuff to Paige's. Why would he want to be at his place, when he could be at hers, where it was cozy and homey—because Paige was there?

The week passed so quickly. He kept reminding himself he had to get honest with Paige before Willow got home. But then, all at once, it was Thursday and he still hadn't said anything.

And then on Friday morning, the day his mother was due home from Mexico, when time was seriously running out, Paige buzzed him in the shop. "I need a few minutes. My office?"

"Something wrong?"

"It's about the property." *Crap.* He and his two other mechanics, Jake Lindell and Billy McClesky, were pulling the original engine from a little bit of automotive history, the first of the muscle cars, a '49 Oldsmobile Rocket 88. "Carter. You there? I've got our Realtor holding on the outside line..."

"Uh. Right here. Sorry." Billy and Jake could manage without him. "I'll be right in."

Dread forming a hot, hard ball in the center of his chest, he got out of his coveralls and cleaned up fast at the sink.

Paige's office door was open. She was still on the phone, but she saw him and gestured him in. He hung back in the doorway, reluctant to find out exactly what was going on, as though by not entering the room, he could somehow forestall the inevitable. "All right," she said—to the Realtor, he assumed. "No, Kelly. Uh-uh. Don't even blame yourself. He *told* you he would let you know if there was another offer. It's on Kritinski that he didn't even bother to give us a chance at it and we didn't find out until now..." Alan Kritinski was the owner of the property on Arrowhead Drive. Or had been, anyway, until Willow made her move. "Yes." Paige slid another glance at Carter. "He's here now. I'll talk it over with him and then we'll let you know what we want to do next... Thanks." She hung up and gave him a distracted frown. "You're lurking. Come in and shut the door."

He obeyed, shoving the door closed behind him, dropping into one of the two chairs that faced her desk. "What's up?" As if he didn't know.

"You won't believe this. Kelly was checking the listings and discovered that the Arrowhead Drive property's been sold—and, Carter, you'll never guess who bought it."

And there it was. Yet another chance to come clean. He opened his mouth to tell all.

Nothing came out.

Paige said, "Carter, you're gaping."

"Uh, yeah. Just surprised." He ought to be ashamed of himself. And he was. But that didn't stop him from asking, "Who bought it?" as if he didn't damn well know.

"Brace yourself."

"Hit me with it."

"Your mother bought it."

"Wow," he said lamely, because he knew he had to say something. "That's bizarre."

Paige shook her head. "I don't get it. What could Willow possibly want with an empty factory building, a big parking lot and some office space?"

"Not a clue," he lied some more. Because why stop now?

She chided, "I told you we should move on it."

"And I guess you were right." He put on a regretful expression. It wasn't all that hard. "Sorry. I screwed up." In more ways than one.

But then Paige smiled. It was a real smile, an easy one. The knot of dread in his chest loosened just a little. She shrugged. "Yeah, but it would have been too late anyway. Willow bought it weeks ago, before Thanksgiving. She must have struck the deal just a day or two after Kritinski turned *us* down."

He rubbed a hand over the back of his head. "She's my own mother and still, I will never understand what drives that woman." That, at least, was true.

Paige nodded. "Totally concur. What was she thinking?"

And that was when it came to him. Right then, as Paige agreed with him about Willow. He finally saw the perfect solution to this sticky problem that had so far only kept sucking him down deeper and deeper into lies and evasions.

It was so simple. He should have thought of it before.

Paige never needed to know.

Willow could give them the property as a wedding present, as promised—and keep her mouth shut about the rest of it.

Everybody wins.

Paige was already moving on to the next supposed

step. "So we'll have to start looking again. I'm sure Kelly can find us something that will work for us."

He spoke up then. "Before you turn the Realtor loose, let me talk with my mother." *And tell her she'd better not say a damn word.*

"What good will that do?"

"What good? You just said it yourself. What possible use could she have for that property?" *Except as a bribe to manipulate her own son?* "Whatever she bought it for, I can probably make her see that we need it more than she does. I'm hoping I can get her to sell it to us for a reasonable price." *A price like, say, nothing.* "So just tell Kelly to hold off until we have more time to think about it."

Paige templed her fingers and swiveled in her chair. "Why not? It's certainly worth a shot."

Chapter Eleven

Carter went straight to his own office off the shop and called the mansion. Estrella told him that Willow wasn't due home until the afternoon.

"Have her call me the minute she gets in?"

"Of course."

He tried Willow's cell. Straight to voice mail. He left a message for her to call him immediately.

And then he waited.

She never called back.

He tried the mansion again at two that afternoon. Estrella said Willow had called to say she'd run into an old friend in Denver and wouldn't be home until the next morning.

"Did you ask her to call me?"

"Of course. She hasn't called you yet?" Estrella sounded apprehensive. "I really did make it clear to her that you wanted to hear from her right away."

He soothed the housekeeper and told her not to worry. "We both know my mother. She does what she wants to do." *And to hell with the rest of us.*

"I'll be glad to call her again and remind her that you're waiting to speak with her."

"No, don't do that. It's not your problem. Thank you, Estrella. I'll take it from here."

He called Willow's cell again. This time he left her a detailed message explaining everything, that Paige knew Willow had bought the property but she didn't know why. And Carter had decided she didn't need to know. His mother was to keep her mouth shut about what she'd been up to. He ended with "And when you get this, call me back right away."

Willow never called.

That evening, Dawn and Molly had their Christmas concert at the high school auditorium. Both girls had solos. Carter and Paige sat close to the stage, and Carter tried to focus on the music, on both Dawn's and Molly's accomplishments. They were talented girls, each headed for great things, he was certain. He tried to forget about his damn mother and her games. He thought he did a pretty good job of that.

But later, when he and Paige were alone in her bedroom, she asked him why he seemed so jumpy. He lied and said he was nervous about the engagement party. She kissed him and promised him it was going to be fun, that they would have a great time.

He hardly slept all night. He kept his cell by the bed with the sound on, so desperate to make things clear to Willow that he didn't care that Paige would hear it when it rang.

He had his lies all lined up. If Paige asked him who

was calling at such a late hour, he planned to groan and gripe that it was Willow, who couldn't be disturbed until ten in the morning, but felt perfectly justified calling other people at any damn time of the day or night. Then he would take it in the other room. And once he'd dealt with his mother, he would get back in bed with Paige and pull her into his arms. If she was still awake and wanted to know what the call was about, he'd tell her the good news: Willow was giving them a killer of a wedding present.

But the phone never rang.

By morning, he felt as if he had ants under his skin, all jumpy and freaked. He did his best to hide it from Paige.

But she saw through him, knew him to his core. She knew that something was really bugging him. She just guessed wrong as to what. She caught his face between her hands and kissed him, slow and sweet, and then promised him that the party was going to be beautiful.

She tried to convince him to stay home from BCC. But he told her he needed to go in, even though he didn't. That was in order that he could take off at lunchtime without Paige knowing he'd gone.

He drove to the mansion, planning a stakeout. He would refuse to leave until he'd talked to Willow and she was on board with the plan.

Estrella answered the door in a chef's apron. Wonderful cooking smells drifted out around her. She said she was very sorry. Willow had called to check in at ten and explained that she wanted to have lunch with her "old friend." She wouldn't be home until five that evening.

"But I have it all under control, I promise you, Carter. Everything will be just right for tonight."

He reassured her, "I know it's going to be great, Estrella, because you're in charge and you are the best."

She beamed. "How nice of you to say—and while you're here, why don't you come in for a minute? Let me show you the table. You can have a look at the menu, take a quick tour through the public rooms. I've rearranged the furniture a bit to make it more comfortable for mingling. Plus, the house does look beautiful all done up for the holidays. And on your mother's instruction, I've stocked the wet bar with several bottles of Veuve Clicquot, which will be on ice when the guests arrive. There's nothing like good champagne to get the guests smiling. Especially when you're celebrating something as important as your engagement to that one special woman you want to spend your whole life with."

He could not have cared less about the menu—which Paige had approved after sharing it with him—or the table or even the fancy champagne. But Estrella was a total sweetheart, stuck on her own getting ready for *his* party. He couldn't refuse her. "I would love to see…everything."

She stepped back and ushered him in. He followed her through the rooms, oohing and aahing over the showy Christmas decorations and the table set with Sondra Bravo's gold candlesticks, monogrammed gold flatware and gold-rimmed dishes. He told Estrella it was all gorgeous. And it was. That table would have passed muster at the Prince's Palace in Montedoro, where his cousin Rory had grown up. And the food? Estrella's meals were always excellent. But she'd outdone herself, with a full-out prime rib feast. She had five large standing rib roasts all trussed up and rubbed with spices, ready to go into the mansion's three large ovens when the time was right.

When he'd seen it all, she walked him back to the

door and he thanked her again for everything. He returned to BCC and worked for another couple of hours.

And then he went home—well, actually, to Paige's house, which had been more a home to him than his own place for a long time now. He greeted the dogs and found Dawn and Molly in the living room, laughing it up, playing the Wii version of "DanceDanceRevolution." He stuck his head in and waved at them. They giggled, returned his wave and went right on dancing.

He made a circuit of the main floor in search of Paige. When he didn't find her, he climbed the stairs. No sign of her up there, either.

So he texted her. Where u @?

She answered right away. Hair & nails. Party, remember?

He wanted her there with him, didn't want to miss a minute he might have with her. Which was paranoid and he knew it. They had the rest of their lives together. I'm home. Miss u.

She sent back a heart smiley and B there in 1 hr.

He took a shower and then stretched out on the bed to wait for her. But his recent sleepless nights caught up with him. He must have dozed off.

When he woke, it was after five. Paige should've been home two hours ago. Mildly freaked, he groped for his phone. But then he realized that someone had settled the spare blanket over him: Paige.

He pushed back the blanket and swung his feet to the floor.

The sound of feminine voices led him to the shut door of Dawn's room. He knocked. "Dawn?"

"Don't come in here! No men allowed!" Dawn yelled back.

"Where's Paige?"

The door opened a crack and Paige stuck her head out. "Right here." Her silky hair was piled up loosely in pretty, soft curls. "Did you sleep well?"

"Great." He bent close and brushed her lips with his. She smelled like roses and some sexy spice, and he wanted her out from behind that door and into his empty arms.

She said, "I'll be out in ten minutes."

He leaned on the doorframe. "Why not now?"

Dawn called, "Eye makeup, Carter! We need Paige for that."

Paige explained, "It seems I have a talent for the gradient effect."

Which told him nothing. "Huh?"

"It'll be more like half an hour," Dawn called. "And the sooner you let her get back in here, the sooner she'll be done!"

So he left them alone and went downstairs, where he ate a handful of peanuts to hold him over until the prime rib and hoped that Paige would hurry. They could maybe slip in a quickie before they finished getting ready.

But when she met him in the bedroom twenty minutes later and he tried to kiss her, she wasn't going for it. "I just spent half the day getting my hair like this. Now you want to me to roll around on the bed with you?"

"Your hair looks beautiful." He eased her robe off her shoulders. "I'll be careful."

"Liar." She pushed his hand away.

He pouted. Even though men don't pout. Unless they have no shame…

"Poor baby." She relented then, and kissed him. And then she stepped back and shook a finger at him. "Don't you even touch my hair."

"I wouldn't. I swear it…"

And then, slowly, she sank to her knees.

Damn, she was amazing. Too many years they'd wasted. He would do anything to keep her, now that he finally had her in the fullest way.

He clasped his hands behind his back to keep them from going where they ached to go—which was directly into all those soft, silky curls. He made himself *not* touch her and watched her use her hands and mouth on him. It was so beautiful. He never wanted it to end.

But it did. Spectacularly. When he pulled her to her feet again, he tried to return the favor. But she only pressed her soft hand to his cheek and said, "We're out of time. I need to get ready."

Out of time. It sounded so…ominous.

Would Ma be back at the mansion now? Maybe he could sneak in a quick call to her.

"Carter?"

"Huh?"

Paige gazed up at him, her smooth brow crinkled in a frown. "You seem distracted. Are you all right?"

"Are you kidding? You just went down on me and I'm getting prime rib for dinner. What could possibly be wrong?"

He did try to reach Willow again on her cell while Paige was busy in the bathroom. Straight to voice mail. He didn't even bother to leave a message. And there was no point in calling the mansion again just to listen to poor, overworked Estrella make excuses for his mother.

Fine. If possible, he'd get Ma alone during the party. If not, well, he just hoped to hell he'd get lucky and she wouldn't tell Paige the real reason she'd bought the property right out from under their noses.

What a mess. His mother was a piece of work—popping up out of nowhere when you didn't want her around, never available when you needed her.

His hair was kind of scrambled after his nap, so he grabbed another quick shower and put on a good suit. Paige looked terrific in a black dress with one of those tops that tied behind her neck and left her pretty shoulders bare. It fit like a glove on top and flared out from the waist to just above her knees. Dawn and Molly were looking excellent, too, in party dresses and high heels. Most of the snow had melted from the week before, so he drove them in the '54 Cadillac sedan he'd restored years ago and had Jake bring over from storage at BCC that afternoon.

The mansion was lit up so bright you could probably see it from Denver. Holiday music flowed from inside. Family and friends were already gathering when he handed the keys to one of the parking attendants hired for the night. He ushered Paige and the girls up the wide white steps and inside where a giant tree blazed in the foyer, and his mother smiled and hugged people and said, "Welcome, welcome. So glad you could come." She wore sparkly white silk and looked half her age.

She hugged him, too. "Darling. You are so handsome. Welcome to your party. I think you'll agree that Estrella has outdone herself."

"We need to talk," he said, low, for her ears alone.

She acted as if she didn't hear him. "Paige!" she exclaimed over his shoulder. "You look just beautiful…"

He told himself to give it up. Now wasn't the time.

But he knew he wouldn't be able to stop himself from watching for his moment.

He filed into the front parlor with everyone else. The

large room was decorated to holiday perfection and the Veuve Clicquot waited on ice. A pretty woman in a red gown at the grand piano sang "Have Yourself a Merry Little Christmas" in a sultry alto voice.

Carter accepted a flute of the champagne and made the rounds, visiting with his brothers and sisters, telling everyone how great it was that they could come, while he kept an eye on his mother, waiting for her to duck out for a minute at the same time as he kept reminding himself that he was totally losing it. If she didn't want to talk to him, he should just let it the hell go.

About seven-thirty, he got lucky. He saw when Willow slipped out of the large parlor and into the foyer.

Paige, across the room laughing and chattering with Clara and Rory, had her back to him. He seized the moment and ducked out after Willow.

As his mother crossed the foyer, he trailed a little ways behind her. She smiled at the guests who lingered near the giant tree, and started up the stairs. He waited until she was at the top and then did the same, waving and nodding as he went by the group of friends around the tree. At the upstairs landing, he saw her ahead, strolling along the upper hallway. He rushed to catch up as she turned the corner into the master suite's private foyer. When he rounded that corner, she'd already crossed the foyer and was entering the suite. He caught up with her just as she was about to close the door.

"Hold on a minute, Ma."

"Carter!" She put her hand to her chest. "You startled me."

"We need to talk and you know that we do."

"Not right now, darling." She tried to close the door

on him. He stuck his foot in it. "Carter. Please. It has to be obvious to you that this is not the time." She kept pushing on the door, but he didn't move his foot.

Fine. It would only take a minute. They didn't need a long conversation. He just wanted her agreement about what *not* to tell Paige. "I know you got my messages," he whispered through the crack his foot was keeping in the door. "You know what I want. Just tell me you understand and you won't say a word to Paige about that little bribe of yours, and I'll leave you alone. My marrying her has zip to do with your ridiculous scheme and you know it."

Willow sighed heavily and let the door drift open. "Darling. I think you need to step back and take a deep breath. We both know that honesty in a relationship is always preferable to secrets and lies. I think you should tell Paige the truth. I really, truly do."

Carter saw red. It took all his willpower not to batter the damn door with his fist. Who was his crazy-ass home-wrecker mother to take the high road about anything?

And then she said, "But all right. I'll keep your secret if that's really how you want it. You may simply tell Paige that I'm thrilled to give you the property as a wedding gift—and leave out all mention of any *bribe*."

Paige had glanced over her shoulder in time to see Carter duck out after Willow.

She'd been worried about him all day. Something was up with him. Something was wrong.

And she had a very strong feeling that whatever it was, it concerned his mother.

Maybe she should have just left him alone to chase after Willow and do…whatever it was he seemed so determined to do. She could ask him about it later, when they were alone.

But she didn't like that he kept lying to her, telling her everything was fine when she knew in her bones that it wasn't.

So she left Clara and Rory chatting together, and followed him as he followed Willow out into the foyer and up the grand staircase.

When he turned a corner at the end of the hallway, she hesitated. Maybe she really should leave this alone, go back downstairs and ask him later what he'd been doing up here. She turned to go—and then couldn't quite give it up.

So much between them was so beautiful. And yet…

She loved him and she'd told him so and he had said nothing.

There were just too many games between them. She wore his ring on her finger, but she wouldn't know if it was real until after the holidays—and a totally ridiculous pro-and-con evaluation.

Uh-uh. She needed to know what was happening here.

She squared her shoulders and kept going, hesitating again at the end of the hallway. From there, she could hear Willow talking tightly about secrets and lies, about honesty in a relationship, about how Paige should know the truth. About the property being a wedding gift.

And how she would never say anything about a bribe.

A bribe? Paige didn't get it.

And she was eavesdropping, plain and simple. That wasn't right.

Anxiety building, her heart suddenly racing, she stepped out from behind the shelter of the wall and directly into a foyer area. About ten feet away, Carter stood with his back to her at a half-open door.

Willow, on the other side of that door, spotted her immediately. "Paige," she said softly, with a strange little smile.

Carter whipped around. The sudden stark misery on his face told Paige way more than she wanted to know. He whispered her name. "Paige…"

And her heart kept on beating frantically, as though it would punch through the wall of her chest. So many lies. Too many silly games. Where even to start?

But she was the levelheaded one, the sane one who never let her emotions get the better of her. So she only asked mildly, "What bribe?"

Carter blanched.

Willow said, "Carter will explain everything." She gave her son another of those weird little smiles. "Won't you, darling?"

Carter just said, "Paige, I…" And then ran out of words.

No drama, Paige reminded herself. No drama, no way. At least not until she had him alone. "How about this? Let's discuss it later. Right now we're the guests of honor at this beautiful party your mom has thrown for us." She held out her hand to him. "Let's go downstairs where we belong."

Paige felt oddly anesthetized for the rest of the evening. As if she were wrapped in gauze, looking at everything through a white fabric screen, feeling everything distantly, as though every inch of her skin had gone numb.

But even numb and wrapped in gauze, she could see that the party was a success. Carter's brothers and sisters all said that the mansion had never looked so warm and inviting, that Estrella had outdone herself.

And Willow, as it turned out, was an excellent hostess—Willow, who spent most of her time traveling, who rarely attended local events and seemed to consider family gatherings dangerous to her health.

Not tonight, not at this party. Tonight, Willow was someone else altogether, happy and chatty, her smile glowing and sincere.

When they took their seats at the table, Willow made a toast to the happy couple. Carter's mom said that she'd known the first time she met Paige, at Bravo Custom Cars three days after Paige had taken the job as office manager, that Paige was the one for her oldest son.

Willow gave a husky chuckle. "Though I have to say, I never would have guessed that it would take the two of them five more years to figure out what I knew the minute I saw them together."

A ripple of knowing laughter filled the room. Everyone seemed to know something Paige didn't really get. Across the table, Dawn and Molly were laughing with everyone else. Dawn leaned close to her best friend and whispered something.

Molly nodded and giggled some more.

Paige remembered the Saturday morning after Thanksgiving, when she'd confided in Dawn, and Dawn had told her that "everyone" knew she had a thing for Carter.

Now Willow was standing right there at the table, lifting a cut crystal champagne flute that had once belonged to her lifelong rival, saying that she'd been waiting five years for Carter and Paige to finally get together. And judging by the nods, the laughter and the grins on all their faces, everyone at the table knew what Willow knew.

They all knew everything.

Only Paige was left stumbling in the dark.

And what about Carter? How much did he know?

She wanted to turn to him and ask him straight out. But now wasn't the time. This wasn't the place. And besides, Paige didn't dare look at him. She had the strangest feeling that, if she looked at him, into his eyes, the numbness would fade and the gauze would fall away.

And she would be left there, seeing too much, every inch of her body burning and tingling in excruciating pain.

Willow continued talking, so relaxed, smiling and gracious. She said she was so glad that her son had figured out what he really wanted at last. She said that she adored her only grandchild, Quinn's daughter, Annabelle. And she wanted more grandchildren, please. She scolded Paige and Carter that they shouldn't take forever about it—she wasn't getting any younger, after all.

Through the rest of the evening, Paige kept her head up. That strange numbness kept her nice and calm as she played her part.

"Okay, what's going on with you two?" Dawn asked as soon as they were back in Carter's gorgeous old Cadillac and on the way home.

"Not a thing," said Carter.

"We're fine," Paige lied.

Dawn made a scoffing sound, but she left it alone. Molly was staying over. Paige dreaded the moment when she and Carter were alone. Things needed to be said and yet she didn't want to say them. And she really didn't want Dawn and Molly around for any of it.

Carter must have felt the same way. When he pulled into the driveway and sent the garage rumbling up, he said, "Paige and I have to go over to my place. You two go on in. We'll see you later."

Dawn leaned up between the seats. "What is going on?"

Paige had no answer for her, so she just said, "Go ahead. We're at Carter's if you need us."

Dawn gave her a long, searching look. Paige's stomach spurted acid as she waited for resistance.

But then Dawn only made a frustrated sound low in her throat and said, "Fine. See you later." She and Molly got out and went in through the garage.

Carter shut the garage door and backed out from the driveway.

Carter's house was cold.

He hadn't been there for weeks, except to grab more of his stuff to take over to Paige's. Even Sally was at Paige's. He hadn't put up any Christmas decorations—but he rarely did. It had always seemed pointless to him to put up a tree and spend all that time decorating it when he was the only one around to look at it and he would rather be at Paige and Dawn's, anyway.

He turned up the heat and asked Paige if she wanted anything. She shook her head and took the couch. He longed to sit beside her. But those fine, dark eyes said he'd better not try it.

He sat in the easy chair across from her.

For an endless five seconds or so, they stared at each other.

Finally, she said, "So tell me. About this *bribe*." She sat so still, her pale, pretty face way too calm. He had the strangest feeling that any second she would shatter.

But she didn't shatter.

Not Paige.

He told her everything, all of it. About the drink he'd had with his mother on Thanksgiving Day when Willow told him she'd bought the property—for him. That she wanted him married and when he *did* get married, the property would be his wedding present from her.

"I would have told you that day." He couldn't keep a hint of bitterness from creeping in. "But you would hardly talk to me. As it turned out, you were freaked over that silly love quiz, remember?"

She reminded him way too softly, "You've had plenty of opportunities since then to tell me all about it."

Something deep inside him twisted. "Yeah. I kept promising myself I would come clean with you. Soon. But, well, *soon* never came. We were together and it was so damn good and I didn't want to rock that boat, didn't want to take a chance I might lose you. I was afraid you wouldn't believe me when I told you that my wanting to marry you had nothing to do with the damn property. And then, the longer I didn't tell you, the harder it got to figure out how to tell you. Finally, the other day, when Kelly called to tell you my mother had bought the property, I..." Damn. He did not want to tell the rest of it. But Paige was waiting. And he knew she wouldn't let him get away with any more lies. "I decided there was no reason you ever had to know the whole story. I decided I would get my mother to do just what she planned to do, give us the property as a wedding present. But as far as her scheme to bribe me into marriage with it went, I would just tell her never to say a word to you about that." He paused for breath—and also, because he was kind of hoping she might say something.

Like maybe, that she understood.

Didn't happen. So he forged on. "Unfortunately, all of a sudden, my mother was unavailable. I kept calling and leaving messages. I even dropped in at the mansion, but she wasn't there. By the time we got to the party, I was frantic to get through to her. So when she went upstairs, I followed her. I caught her at the door to her room and I told her what I wanted from her. And could she just agree to do it my way? Oh, hell, no. Suddenly, she was all about honesty and how lies weren't a good foundation for a relationship. You walked in on her telling me that." He put up both hands. "And that's it. That's all of it. It was stupid and I was wrong and all I want is for us to get past this."

Paige drew a very slow breath. "Carter." She turned her head and stared into the dark fireplace. "I just..." Another slow breath. It seemed to be a huge effort for her, but she made herself look at him again. "I don't want to do this anymore."

He pretended not to understand. He couldn't *bear* to understand. "What are you talking about? Come on. You have to believe me. The property doesn't have a damn thing to do with why I want to marry you."

She smiled then. He'd never seen her look so sad. "I believe you."

Hope blazed in his chest, searing like a brand. "You do? Thank God." He stood to go to her.

She put out a hand. "No. Please. Don't."

He didn't get it. But his knees did, apparently. They bent and he sank back in to his seat. What was the problem, then? She'd just said she believed him. But still, she was pushing him away. He tried to make it clearer. "I didn't want to lose you. That's all it was…"

"Oh, Carter. Why can't you see? This thing with the property, this big secret you've been keeping from me, it's not the main issue, it's more the final straw. The problem is that I love you. And I went ahead with your ridiculous test-drive marriage plan thinking that somehow I would get you to love me, too. But you…you hold back. You know you do."

Okay, he got it now. And he didn't like it one damn bit. "This is all about *I love you*, isn't it?" he accused. "This is all just because I won't say the silly words." It came out angry. Because, damn it, he was getting mad.

And she just wouldn't cop to it. "No. It's not that. It's really not."

Bull. "Who's lying now?"

"I'm not lying. The words you won't say are just the symptom of the deeper problem. I've seen a true and happy marriage. My parents had one. I want that, what my parents had, I do. And I'm afraid I'll never have that with you."

He was getting that feeling. Like his head might explode. Like his heart might just crash its way out of his chest. "Don't talk to me about symptoms, about how perfect your parents were. This is about *us*, damn it.

About how good it's been since you finally agreed to wear my ring. You *know* how good it's been. I know you know. You and me, together, it's better than I ever dreamed it could be."

"Well, it's not good enough for me."

He wanted to yell at her, to shout the house down. But he kept it together, just barely. He braced his elbows on his spread knees and leaned across the table at her. "What in the hell do you want from me, Paige?"

She pressed her own knees together, planted her elbows on them and leaned right back at him. "What do I want? Well, let's see. How 'bout a *real* engagement? How about, if you're going to ask me to marry you, you do it straight out and let me say yes or no? You don't come up with some bat-crap-crazy idea about trying it out until the holidays are over and then *evaluating* the *situation* to see if we want to make it real or we don't."

Okay, yeah. Maybe the test-drive hadn't been such a great idea. And he should apologize some more, he knew it. He should drop to his knees and beg. Because it would kill him to lose her and she had a right to know the whole truth, the one he'd been hiding from her—and from himself—for eight damn years.

But he didn't beg. He was too furious at her. "What else was I supposed to do?"

She gasped as though he'd just said something so outrageous. And then she whispered hotly, "I just told you, you need to say what you want, to be honest about it."

"Honest. Right."

"Don't you mock me, Carter."

"How can I help it? You're so full of crap. All your talk about being honest, as though it's so simple. Just tell Paige what you want from her. Just be honest and straightforward. Yeah, sure. You mean like I was honest eight years ago when I first met you? Because I *was* honest and we both know it. I went right after what I wanted, and it was you. And you had one answer for me back then. That answer was no. You turned me down. Repeatedly."

"That was all I *could* do right then," she cried. "I'd just lost my parents. My fiancé, the guy who'd said he loved me more than his life, had dumped me flat the second things got tough. I had a little sister to raise. I wasn't in any condition to be going out on *dates*."

"Yeah. I got that. You wanted a *friend*. And I gave you what you wanted for eight long years. I went out with *strangers*, tried to make it work with women who ended up hating me because I wasn't really there for them. I even succeeded in convincing myself that I wanted what *you* wanted—for you and me to be good buddies, the best of friends. And then, a few weeks ago, with a nudge from my crazy mother and another from Murray Preble, I started to see the light, to admit again what *I* wanted. And it was still you. And so I went after you. And maybe I did it in a roundabout way. Maybe I did go about it all wrong, coming up with a test drive and then an evaluation. Because you're all about the damn pros and cons, Paige, now, aren't you? I thought, well, she can have one of her lists at the end and maybe then she'll finally see that we should be together, maybe she'll…" The words dribbled off into nothing and he was left wondering what the hell was the matter with him?

God help him. He was babbling like an idiot, revealing things he'd never let himself think all that hard about. They hurt, those things. He wished he hadn't said them.

So he shut up. He shut up and he stared at her across that low table, stared long and hard.

She stared back. She looked as if he'd punched her a good one right in the solar plexus, as if he'd knocked all the air clean out of her. "I don't… I just never…" She flopped back against the cushions, then strained forward again. "Oh, Carter, how could you not have known you didn't need that silly test-drive? I told you right out I'm in love with you."

"Oh, come on. Like talking about love is going to make anything clear to me. How many times have I told you that when people talk about love, all I see is my mother standing in the middle of the street, screaming at my dad while he peels rubber to get away from her? All I see is her crying and carrying on, wailing about how much she *loves* him—as she empties his underwear drawer onto the front lawn."

A low whimper escaped Paige. She covered her face with her hands. "Oh, God. What a mess…"

His head pounded in rhythm with his racing heart. He slapped a hand on the back of his neck and squeezed, hard, as though he could rub the pain away. "Terrific. This is a big mess and I'm still a liar, right? That's all you can see."

She dropped her hands and gaped at him. "No. That's not what I said. Carter, can we just dial it down a notch? I just need a little time to—"

"Stop." He lurched upright. "Just don't, okay?" He felt like someone had taken a belt sander to his heart. Everybody thought love was so damn great. He failed to see the wonderfulness. It just felt like torture to him. "I'm taking you home."

"But we need to—"

"No. No, we don't. I've had enough, okay? I get it now, Paige. It's not going to work with us. You've made that way clear. I want this to be done."

She stood, too, then, slowly. Her big eyes brimmed with tears. "What, exactly, are you saying?" She whispered those words.

"I'm saying you're right. Us, getting married? Dumb idea." He was lying. But what did it matter, whether he lied or told the truth? Either way, she refused to believe him. Either way, he'd messed everything up completely. They might as well get it over with. He might as well just do what she expected of him. "I want to take you home, pick up my dog and move on."

She looked at him so hard. As if those big eyes could bore a hole in the center of his forehead. Her soft mouth quivered. But she didn't say anything. He wanted to grab her and hold on so tight, she would never think of leaving him again.

But he just couldn't take it. All this hurt, all this *feeling*. This wasn't going to work. And he needed to end it. Now.

So he did. "Let's just stay away from each other until after the holidays. Tell you what. Don't come in Monday. Take a couple of weeks' vacation, why don't you? And then at the first of the year, we'll take a meeting, talk about BCC and whether or not it's really workable for you and me to be partners anymore."

She sucked in a shocked breath. He waited for her to argue, to do something impossible. Like maybe to fight for what they had.

But she didn't.

He watched, hating himself, already starting to see all the ways he'd blown it, as she took off his ring and set it carefully on the coffee table. "All right, Carter," she said. "Take me home now."

Chapter Twelve

At Paige's house, Carter waited outside.

Paige went in alone. The house was quiet. The light under Dawn's door meant the girls were probably still awake.

Quietly—so they wouldn't hear her, come out to investigate and start asking questions—Paige gathered up everything she could find of Carter's and stuck it in a duffel she dug out of the closet. Then she put Sally on her leash and took the dog and the duffel out the front door.

He was waiting for her, leaning against the driver's door of the Cadillac, making her ache with yearning just at the sight of him. He accepted the big bag from her and went to toss it in the trunk as she put Sally in the backseat. Then he slid in behind the wheel again. She stood in the driveway and watched his taillights until he turned the corner and they disappeared.

Inside, Biscuit was waiting by the front door. She took

him out for a few minutes, then let him come upstairs with her. He hogged the bed, as usual. He also cuddled up close and tried to lick the tears off her cheeks as she cried.

The next morning, when the girls came downstairs and asked where Carter was, Paige played it vague. "He, um, decided to spend the night at his house."

Dawn made a groaning sound low in her throat. "Have you *looked* in the mirror? You've been crying all night, haven't you—and where's your ring?"

The tears crept up the back of Paige's throat again and filled her eyes. "We're, um, having some problems. Taking a little break, is all."

Dawn wasn't buying that. "He broke up with you. That idiot. I'll kill him."

"No!" It came out on a sob. "It's at least as much my fault as his."

"No way."

"Yeah. It really is. I hurt him. I've *been* hurting him for a very long time. And I…oh, Dawn. I think we both really blew it and I don't know what's going to happen. He said it's over. He really seemed to mean it."

Dawn grabbed her and hugged her as Biscuit moved close and whimpered in sympathy. "I'll kill him," Dawn threatened in her ear.

"Don't say that. I love him."

"I know you do."

"I'll always love him. And…and *he* loves *me*, even though he can never make himself say it."

"Oh, Paige. I know that, too."

A laugh that was more like a sob escaped her. "Because everybody knows, right?"

"Yeah, pretty much."

Paige held on tight, breathing in the familiar smell of Dawn's strawberry shampoo, grateful beyond measure that she had her sister to hold on to.

Molly got up and joined the hug, too. The three of them just stood there in the kitchen, holding on to each other, as Paige let go and cried even harder than she had the night before, and Biscuit whimpered at their feet.

Later, when they sat down to Molly's special German pancakes, Paige told the girls what she'd planned. "Carter gave me vacation time till the first of the year. And I'm going to take it. I'm calling an old college friend, a travel agent, tomorrow. I'm seeing if I can book a last-minute trip to someplace where I can sit on a beach in the sun in the yellow bikini I bought last summer and never took the tags off of. I want to leave right away and I'll be back by New Year's, in time for your spring semester. Either of you want to go?"

Dawn and Molly exchanged a look. Dawn nodded. "I'm in."

And Molly said, "I'll call my mom and see if it's okay."

Carter was at the shop, alone, that afternoon, when Dawn pounded on the side door.

He let her in and then he grabbed her in a hug. She didn't seem to care if he got grease all over her, just hugged him back as hard as he was hugging her.

When she pulled away, she clutched his shoulders and glared up at him. "God, Carter. You look as miserable as she is."

What was he supposed to say to that? He settled for saying nothing.

Not Dawn. "I told you I'd kill you. I still kind of want to. I mean, all guys are stupid a lot of the time.

But you… I don't get it. Paige won't really talk about it. What *happened*?"

"I screwed it up."

"Well, then fix it."

He pulled free of her grip. "Just let it go, Dawnie. Just, you know, let it be, huh?"

"We're leaving, Paige and me and Molly."

"Huh? Going where?"

"I don't know yet, but we'll be gone until New Year's. Paige won't ask you, so I will. Would you take care of Biscuit while we're gone?"

"Of course."

"You should call her."

"Stay out of it, Dawn."

She pressed her lips together and muttered, "You are the king of stupid and I have zero sympathy for you."

Paige's college friend worked a miracle, though at a premium price. It was high season, but still, they got a two-bedroom bungalow in a resort on Saint John, Virgin Islands.

Dawn took Biscuit to Carter's on Monday night. When she got back to the house, Paige demanded, "Did you tell him where we're going?"

Dawn shrugged. "He didn't ask and I wasn't about to volunteer anything."

"Good," Paige replied, and tried to sound as though she meant it.

They left before daylight the next morning. Snow was falling when they boarded the plane in Denver.

On Saint John, it was eighty degrees under a cloudless sky, the sun beaming down on the blue ocean and the sparkly white sand. Paige got out her yellow bikini and cut off the tags and tried to care that she'd soon be basking in the Caribbean sun.

In Justice Creek, Carter shoveled his front walk and hung out with Biscuit and Sally. He wasn't good for much else.

In that final week before Christmas, business was kind of slow. A good thing, because for the first time since he was thirteen and Dobs Kelvin, the old biker who lived down the street, put a wrench in his hand, Carter couldn't work on his cars. They reminded him of Paige.

But then, everything reminded him of Paige. He had it so bad. Worse, even, than he'd realized on Saturday when he told her he was cutting her loose.

Cutting her loose.

Yeah, right. And while he was at it, he might as well cut out his heart.

And come to think of it, he kind of had.

Now that the fury had faded, he was starting to see the truth.

And it wasn't pretty.

He was worse than Willow had been back in the day. He might as well have emptied Paige's underwear drawer in the street, the way he'd carried on Saturday night, threatening to bust up their partnership at BCC, blaming her for all the times he didn't make it work with other women…

He wanted to go to her so bad.

But she was gone and he had no idea where to find her.

On Wednesday, he left the shop early and went to Romano's for dinner. He ordered the veal piccata, which was excellent, as always, though he barely managed to choke down a few bites. Because, come on. Who did he think he was kidding, to try to eat dinner at the restaurant where he'd met Paige?

Murray and Sherry were there, sitting in a booth in the corner, eyes only for each other. He wanted to be happy for them. But he kept asking himself why they got to be happy and he had to lose everything that mattered most.

Because you're the king of stupid, Dawn's voice echoed in his ear.

On Christmas Eve, his cousin Rory married Walker McKellan in a rustic chapel in the national forest. Carter went because he couldn't think of an acceptable excuse not to. Rory's parents, the sovereign princess and prince consort of Montedoro, were there. It was a beautiful setting, and the bride and groom looked so happy, and that just made Carter feel worse than ever.

His brothers and sisters asked him where Paige was. He said he didn't know. They all wisely left it at that—well, except for Nell. She took him aside and told him he was crazy if he'd let Paige go.

He told her to mind her own damn business.

She grabbed his arm and whispered, "Carter. Don't blow this. Don't throw away what matters most to you."

"Leave it, Nell." He jerked his arm free and got the hell away from her.

On Christmas Day, he got the visit he'd been dreading, the one from his mother. She came at seven in the morning, which shocked the hell out of him. He'd never actually seen her awake at that hour.

Willow told him she was giving him and Paige the property as a Christmas present. She petted the dogs and said gently, "Nothing is unfixable."

He admitted the disgusting truth. "I acted like a drama queen."

And his mother smiled. "Well, at least you come by it naturally."

"It's not funny, Ma."

"I never said it was. Now get your ass to wherever she's run off to, admit how wrong you were and tell her you're not leaving until she comes home with you."

He opened his mouth to order her out of his house. But the words that came out were "I messed up on so many levels. She's probably never going to speak to me again."

Willow hugged him. That was seriously weird. "She loves you and you love her," she said softly when he saw her to the door. "I know you'll work it out."

Half an hour later, he sat on the couch with Biscuit on one side and Sally on the other, channel-surfing like mad and telling himself that Paige *had* to come back eventually. She had a house and a dog—and Dawn and Molly had school.

His phone trilled three notes: incoming text.

It was from Dawn. She still loves you, you idiot. You need to come here and work it out.

The address of a luxury resort in the Virgin Islands followed, complete with a bungalow number.

At eight the next morning, it was seventy-two degrees on Saint John and the sun was shining bright.

Carter, his heart banging like a gong in the prison of his chest, stood at the door to Paige's bungalow and lifted his hand to knock.

The door swung open before his knuckles made contact.

Paige. She wore a gauzy sky-blue shirt that came to

midthigh. Her hair needed combing. Her cheeks were pink from the sun and she'd sprouted a few freckles across her adorable nose.

"My God," he said prayerfully. He'd never seen anything so beautiful in his life.

She scowled at him—but her eyes were shining. "What did you do with my dog?"

"My mother's looking after both Biscuit and Sally. Believe it or not, she's good with them. She also gave us the property as a Christmas present."

"Us? I thought there was no us. I thought you just wanted to be done."

"I lied."

She said nothing, only gazed up at him, waiting.

He knew he owed her more, so damn much more. "I… you were right. I messed everything up with that stupid test-drive engagement. I never wanted that. I was just afraid that if I came right out and asked you for forever, you might turn me down. And then I didn't tell you about my mother trying to bribe me with the property, because I was scared I'd lose you over that. Then the night of our party, when all my lies came back to bite me in the ass, I lied some more and told you I was through. That was the biggest lie, Paige. Because for me, you're the one. I'll never be through with you."

She swallowed. Hard. "I've lied, too—to myself. About you. About who you really are to me. I should have opened my eyes to the truth sooner. Jim Kellogg hurt me and I held on to that hurt for way too long."

"Are you…over that now?"

"I am, Carter. I really am."

"Ahem. Well, then. I know it's a lot to ask. Maybe too much to ask. Because I know I blew it, and I'm so sorry that I did. But still, I want to try again. I would give anything, if you and I could try again."

Her face seemed to light right up from within. "My mom always used to say it's not how bad you mess up, it's how hard you work to heal the pain you cause each other."

"I'm…I'm willing Paige. Whatever it takes, I'll do it. For you."

Her sweet mouth trembled. "I'm willing, too, Carter. For you."

"Paige?"

"Um?"

"I just need to get my arms around you."

She made a tight little sound, as if her throat had locked up on her. Her shining eyes had tears in them now. "Well, um, you'd better do that, then."

"Dear God. Yes." And he reached out and hauled her close, splaying his hands across her slender back, burying his face in the crook of her neck, loving the feel of her, so soft in all the right places, drinking in the scent of her, like soap and vanilla.

Like home.

"You're my home, Paige," he whispered idiotically.

"Carter." She pressed those sweet lips to the side of his throat. "I love you. I missed you so. I'm so sorry, that I couldn't be…with you sooner. I'm so sorry I hurt you, that I didn't understand."

He made his own confession. "I didn't let you see, didn't tell you the truth. I wanted you so much and I worked so hard for so long to tell myself that being your friend was enough. And in some ways, it was. It really was. It was a whole hell of a lot better than not having you at all. But…" His mind was a fog, with jet lag and longing, with the unbelievable wonder of her right there, breath and flesh and heart and soul, all held at last in his hungry arms.

She pulled back and looked up him through those big, misty eyes. “It’s okay. You don’t have to—”

He put a finger to her lips. “Yeah. I have to. I need to say it. I need you to know that I do love you, that I always have. That I walked into Romano’s that night eight years ago and I saw you standing there with an order book in your hand, wearing that white shirt and that short black skirt and that little triangle of an apron, with your hair pulled up in a knot on the top of your head, laughing at something a customer had said. I took one look at you and I thought, *Oh, yeah. Mine. I’ll take her for the rest of my life...*”

She scanned his face, drinking him in, as though she’d been wandering in the desert and he was made of water. “Carter. You said it.”

“Yeah, I did. And I’ll say it again. I love you. You’re the woman for me, Paige. You’re the only one.” He pulled her close again and he kissed her.

She let him kiss her.

She more than let him. She wrapped her arms good and tight around him and she lifted that soft, fine mouth to his.

When he raised his head, she took his hand.

He grabbed the suitcase he’d dropped on the step and let her lead him inside, through a simply furnished, sunlit living area, down a short hall to the open door of a bedroom.

“Dawn and Molly?” he asked.

“In the other bedroom, still sleeping.” She entered the

room and pulled him in with her, pausing only to quietly shut the door and turn the privacy lock.

He barely had time to set the suitcase down again before she got to work unbuttoning his shirt. "I love you," he said as she undressed him. "I love you so much, Paige. I thought I would lose you. I couldn't work, couldn't sleep—"

"Shh. You haven't lost me. You never could. Not really. We would always find our way back to each other in the end."

And then she kissed him again and they fell across the bed together.

Make-up sex. Nothing like it.

Especially make-up sex with love, spoken freely, given honestly.

An hour later, she put her blue shirt back on and he got dressed again. They went out to the tiny galley kitchen. He made coffee.

"So good," she said, when she took that first sip. "Nobody makes it like you do." She let him fill his own cup, then led him outside to the small private lanai with its own perfect view of white sand and blue ocean.

They shared a chaise. It was cramped, but neither of them could bear not to be touching the other.

He held her close against him and drew lazy figure eights on the velvety skin of her arm. "Remember the love quiz?"

She groaned, "How will I ever forget? That was awful. It really was, Carter. You have to understand, it hit me hard, to realize out of the blue that I'm in love with you. And that I probably have been for a very long time. And I had no hope at all then that *you* might love *me* that way."

He gave a pained laugh. "But I did love you that way. I'd just been telling myself not to go there for eight long years."

"Because of me, because for so long that was all I could handle, for us to be just friends."

"Exactly—and didn't you ever wonder how I got twenty out of twenty to 'prove' you were in love with me?"

She turned in his arms, so she was half lying on his chest. And she pressed a kiss on the end of his chin. "I just thought it was what you told me, that you knew me so well, you'd guessed and you'd guessed right."

"Wrong."

"Well, okay. Then what?"

"There was no guessing involved." He cradled the side of her face, ran his hand down the length of her warm, silky hair. "Those answers were *my* answers. Twenty out of twenty."

She sighed. And then she tucked her head under his chin. "*Your* answers. I never had a clue…"

He kissed the top of her head. "Happy day-after-Christmas."

She snuggled in closer. "I missed you so much yesterday. Dawn and I agreed it was hardly like Christmas, without you standing at the counter mixing stuffing at the crack of dawn, getting the turkey ready to go in the oven. We left all the presents, untouched, under the tree at home…"

"When we get back, I'll roast a turkey," he promised. "We'll have Christmas all over again."

"And we'll do it right this time." She laid her hand over his heart. "Is it snowing in Justice Creek?"

"It was when I left."

"I missed that, snow for Christmas..."

He ran a hand down the sweet curve of her back. And then he asked, low and rough, for her ears alone, "Will you please come back to me, Paige? Will you give me one more chance? Come back and be my wife and my best friend and my partner at BCC. I swear to you that I'll never lie to you again, never hide the truth no matter how painful the truth might be, no matter how bad it makes me look. I'll never make a game of loving you, never hold you at a distance by not showing you my heart. Because you're everything to me, Paige. And life without you is nothing but a gray, depressing slog."

"Yes," she whispered without hesitation. "Yes, I will marry you and be your wife, your best friend and your business partner for the rest of our lives. Because you are the man for me, Carter Bravo. And no one else will do."

A long, coffee-flavored kiss sealed the deal.

After the kiss, he pulled her to her feet, slipped his ring back on her finger and took her into the bungalow, where they woke the girls and shared the news that they would be spending the rest of their lives together, after all.

* * * * *

Watch for JAMES BRAVO'S SHOTGUN BRIDE,
the next installment in Christine Rimmer's
THE BRAVOS OF JUSTICE CREEK *miniseries*
coming in May 2016,
only from Harlequin Special Edition.

SPECIAL EXCERPT FROM

When oilman Blair Coleman and the much younger Niki Ashton fall for one another, can the two overcome tragedy to find forever in each other's arms?

Read on for a sneak preview of WYOMING RUGGED, the latest WYOMING MEN *tale from* New York Times *bestselling author Diana Palmer.*

SHE SIGHED. HE was very handsome. She loved the way his eyes crinkled when he smiled. She loved the strong, chiseled lines of his wide mouth, the high cheekbones, the thick black wavy hair around his leonine face. His chest was a work of art in itself. She had to force herself not to look at it too much. It was broad and muscular, under a thick mat of curling black hair that ran down to the waistband of his silk pajamas. Apparently, he didn't like jackets, because he never wore one with the bottoms. His arms were muscular, without being overly so. He would have delighted an artist.

"What are you thinking so hard about?" he wondered aloud.

"That an artist would love painting you," she blurted out, and then flushed then cleared her throat. "Sorry. I wasn't thinking."

He lifted both eyebrows. "Miss Ashton," he scoffed, "you aren't by any chance flirting with me, are you?"

"Mr. Coleman, the thought never crossed my mind!"

"Don't obsess over me," he said firmly, but his eyes were still twinkling. "I'm a married man."

She sighed. "Yes, thank goodness."

His eyebrows lifted in a silent question.

"Well, if you weren't married, I'd probably disgrace myself. Imagine, trying to ravish a sick man in bed because I'm obsessing over the way he looks without a shirt!"

He burst out laughing. "Go away, you bad girl."

Her own eyes twinkled. "I'll banish myself to the kitchen and make lovely things for you to eat."

"I'll look forward to that."

She smiled and left him.

He looked after her with conflicting emotions. He had a wife. Sadly, one who was a disappointment in almost every way; a cold woman who took and took without a thought of giving anything back. He'd married her thinking she was the image of his mother. Elise had seemed very different while they were dating. But the minute the ring was on her finger, she was off on her travels, spending more and more of his money, linking up with old friends whom she paid to travel with her. She was never home. In fact, she made a point of avoiding her husband as much as possible.

This really was the last straw, though, ignoring him when he was ill. It had cut him to the quick to have Todd and Niki see the emptiness of their relationship. He wasn't that sick. It was the principle of the thing. Well, he had some thinking to do when he left the Ashtons, didn't he?

CHRISTMAS DAY WAS BOISTEROUS. Niki and Edna and three other women took turns putting food on the table for an unending succession of people who worked for the Ashtons. Most were cowboys, but several were executives from Todd's oil corporation.

Niki liked them all, but she was especially fond of their children. She dreamed of having a child of her own one day. She spent hours in department stores, ogling the baby things.

She got down on the carpet with the children around the Christmas tree, oohing and aahing over the presents as they opened them. One little girl who was six years old got a Barbie doll with a holiday theme. The child cried when she opened the gaily wrapped package.

"Lisa, what's wrong, baby?" Niki cooed, drawing her into her lap.

"Daddy never buys me dolls, and I love dolls so much, Niki," she whispered. "Thank you!" She kissed Niki and held on tight.

"You should tell him that you like dolls, sweetheart," Niki said, hugging her close.

"I did. He bought me a big yellow truck."

"A what?"

"A truck, Niki," the child said with a very grown-up sigh. "He wanted a little boy. He said so."

Niki looked as indignant as she felt. But she forced herself to smile at the child. "I think little girls are very sweet," she said softly, brushing back the pretty dark hair.

"So do I," Blair said, kneeling down beside them. He smiled at the child, too. "I wish I had a little girl."

"You do? Honest?" Lisa asked, wide-eyed.

"Honest."

She got up from Niki's lap and hugged the big man. "You're nice."

He hugged her back. It surprised him, how much he wanted a child. He drew back, the smile still on his face. "So are you, precious."

"I'm going to show Mama my doll," she said. "Thanks, Niki!"

"You're very welcome."

The little girl ran into the dining room, where the adults were finishing dessert.

"Poor thing," Niki said under her breath. "Even if he thinks it, he shouldn't have told her."

"She's a nice child," he said, getting to his feet. He looked down at Niki. "You're a nice child, yourself."

She made a face at him. "Thanks. I think."

His dark eyes held an expression she'd never seen before. They fell to her waistline and jerked back up. He turned away. "Any more coffee going? I'm sure mine's cold."

"Edna will have made a new pot by now," she said. His attitude disconcerted her. Why had he looked at her that way? Her eyes followed him as he strode back into the dining room, towering over most of the other men. The little girl smiled up at him, and he ruffled her hair.

He wanted children. She could see it. But apparently his wife didn't. What a waste, she thought. What a wife he had. She felt sorry for him. He'd said when he was engaged that he was crazy about Elise. Why didn't she care enough to come when he was ill?

"It's not my business," she told herself firmly.

It wasn't. But she felt very sorry for him just the same. If he'd married *her*, they'd have a houseful of children.

She'd take care of him and love him and nurse him when he was sick…she pulled herself up short. He was a married man. She shouldn't be thinking such things.

SHE'D BOUGHT PRESENTS online for her father and Edna and Blair. She was careful to get Blair something impersonal. She didn't want his wife to think she was chasing him or anything. She picked out a tie tac, a *fleur de lis* made of solid gold. She couldn't understand why she'd chosen such a thing. He had Greek ancestry, as far as she knew, not French. It had been an impulse.

Her father had gone to answer the phone, a call from a business associate who wanted to wish him happy holidays, leaving Blair and Niki alone in the living room by the tree. She felt like an idiot for making the purchase.

Now Blair was opening the gift, and she ground her teeth together when he took the lid off the box and stared at it with wide, stunned eyes.

"I'm sorry," she began self-consciously. "The sales slip is in there," she added. "You can exchange it if…"

He looked at her. His expression stopped her tirade midsentence. "My mother was French," he said quietly. "How did you know?"

She faltered. She couldn't manage words. "I didn't. It was an impulse."

His big fingers smoothed over the tie tac. "In fact, I had one just like it that she bought me when I graduated from college." He swallowed. Hard. "Thanks."

"You're very welcome."

His dark eyes pinned hers. "Open yours now."

She fumbled with the small box he'd had hidden in his suitcase until this morning. She tore off the ribbons and opened it. Inside was the most beautiful brooch she'd ever seen. It was a golden orchid on an ivory background. The orchid was purple with a yellow center, made of delicate amethyst and topaz and gold.

She looked at him with wide, soft eyes. "It's so beautiful…"

He smiled with real affection. "It reminded me of you, when I saw it in the jewelry store," he lied, because he'd had it commissioned by a noted jewelry craftsman, just for her. "Little hothouse orchid," he teased.

She flushed. She took the delicate brooch out of its box and pinned it to the bodice of her black velvet dress. "I've never had anything so lovely," she faltered. "Thank you."

He stood up and drew her close to him. "Thank you, Niki." He bent and started to brush her mouth with his, but forced himself to deflect the kiss to her soft cheek. "Merry Christmas."

She felt the embrace to the nails of her toes. He smelled of expensive cologne and soap, and the feel of that powerful body so close to hers made her vibrate inside. She was flustered by the contact, and uneasy because he was married.

She laughed, moving away. "I'll wear it to church every Sunday," she promised without really looking at him.

He cleared his throat. The contact had affected him, too. "I'll wear mine to board meetings, for a lucky charm," he teased gently. "To ward off hostile takeovers."

"I promise it will do the job," she replied, and grinned.

Her father came back to the living room, and the sudden, tense silence was broken. Conversation turned to politics and the weather, and Niki joined in with forced cheerfulness.

But she couldn't stop touching the orchid brooch she'd pinned to her dress.

TIME PASSED. BLAIR'S visits to the ranch had slowed until they were almost nonexistent. Her father said Blair was trying to make his marriage work. Niki thought, privately, that it would take a miracle to turn fun-loving Elise into a housewife. But she forced herself not to dwell on it. Blair was married. Period. She did try to go out more with her friends, but never on a blind date again. The experience with Harvey had affected her more than she'd realized.

Graduation day came all too soon. Niki had enjoyed college. The daily commute was a grind, especially in the harsh winter, but thanks to Tex, who could drive in snow and ice, it was never a problem. Her grade point average was good enough for a magna cum laude award. And she'd already purchased her class ring months before.

"Is Blair coming with Elise, do you think?" Niki asked her father as they parted inside the auditorium just before the graduation ceremony.

He looked uncomfortable. "I don't think so," he said. "They've had some sort of blowup," he added. "Blair's butler, Jameson, called me last night. He said Blair locked himself in his study and won't come out."

"Oh, dear," Niki said, worried. "Can't he find a key and get in?"

"I'll suggest that," he promised. He forced a smile. "Go graduate. You've worked hard for this."

She smiled. "Yes, I have. Now all I have to do is decide if I want to go on to graduate school or get a job."

"A job?" he scoffed. "As if you'll ever need to work."

"You're rich," she pointed out. "I'm not."

"You're rich, too," he argued. He bent and kissed her cheek, a little uncomfortably. He wasn't a demonstrative man. "I'm so proud of you, honey."

"Thanks, Daddy!"

"Don't forget to turn the tassel to the other side when the president hands you your diploma."

"I won't forget."

THE CEREMONY WAS LONG, and the speaker was tedious. By the time he finished, the audience was restless, and Niki just wanted it over with.

She was third in line to get her diploma. She thanked the dean, whipped her tassel to the other side as she walked offstage and grinned to herself, imagining her father's pleased expression.

It took a long time for all the graduates to get through the line, but at last it was over, and Niki was outside with her father, congratulating classmates and working her way to the parking lot.

She noted that, when they were inside the car, her father was frowning.

"I turned my tassel," she reminded him.

He sighed. "Sorry, honey. I was thinking about Blair."

Her heart jumped. "Did you call Jameson?"

"Yes. He finally admitted that Blair hasn't been sober for three days. Apparently, the divorce is final, and Blair found out some unsavory things about his wife."

"Oh, dear." She tried not to feel pleasure that Blair

was free. He'd said often enough that he thought of Niki as a child. "What sort of things?"

"I can't tell you, honey. It's very private stuff."

She drew in a long breath. "We should go get him and bring him to the ranch," she said firmly. "He shouldn't be on his own in that sort of mood."

He smiled softly. "You know, I was just thinking the same thing. Call Dave and have them get the Learjet over here. You can come with me if you like."

"Thanks."

He shrugged. "I might need the help," he mused. "Blair gets a little dangerous when he drinks, but he'd never hit a woman," he added.

She nodded. "Okay."

BLAIR DIDN'T RESPOND to her father's voice asking him to open the door. Muffled curses came through the wood, along with sounds of a big body bumping furniture.

"Let me try," Niki said softly. She rapped on the door. "Blair?" she called.

There was silence, followed by the sound of footsteps coming closer. "Niki?" came a deep, slurred voice.

"Yes, it's me."

He unlocked the door and opened it. He looked terrible. His face was flushed from too much alcohol. His black, wavy hair was ruffled. His blue shirt, unbuttoned and untucked, looking as if he'd slept in it. So did his black pants. He was a little unsteady on his feet. His eyes roved over Niki's face with warm affection.

She reached out and caught his big hand in both of hers. "You're coming home with us," she said gently. "Come on, now."

"Okay," he said, without a single protest.

Jameson, standing to one side, out of sight, sighed with relief. He grinned at her father.

Blair drew in a long breath. "I'm pretty drunk."

"That's okay," Niki said, still holding tight to his hand. "We won't let you drive."

He burst out laughing. "Damned little brat," he muttered.

She grinned at him.

"You dressed up to come visit me?" he asked, looking from her to her father.

"It was my graduation today," Niki said.

Blair grimaced. "Damn! I meant to come. I really did. I even got you a present." He patted his pockets. "Oh, hell, it's in my desk. Just a minute."

He managed to stagger over to the desk without falling. He dredged out a small wrapped gift. "But you can't open it until I'm sober," he said, putting it in her hands.

"Oh. Well, okay," she said. She cocked her head. "Are you planning to have to run me down when I open it, then?"

His eyes twinkled. "Who knows?"

"We'd better go before he changes his mind," her father said blithely.

"I won't," Blair promised. "There's too damned much available liquor here. You only keep cognac and Scotch whiskey," he reminded his friend.

"I've had Edna hide the bottles, though," her father assured him.

"I've had enough anyway."

"Yes, you have. Come on," Niki said, grabbing Blair's big hand in hers.

He followed her like a lamb, not even complaining at

her assertiveness. He didn't notice that Todd and Jameson were both smiling with pure amusement.

WHEN THEY GOT back to Catelow, and the Ashton ranch, Niki led Blair up to the guest room and set him down on the big bed.

"Sleep," she said, "is the best thing for you."

He drew in a ragged breath. "I haven't slept for days," he confessed. "I'm so tired, Niki."

She smoothed back his thick, cool black hair. "You'll get past this," she said with a wisdom far beyond her years. "It only needs time. It's fresh, like a raw wound. You have to heal until it stops hurting so much."

He was enjoying her soft hand in his hair. Too much. He let out a long sigh. "Some days I feel my age."

"You think you're old?" she chided. "We've got a cowhand, Mike, who just turned seventy. Know what he did yesterday? He learned to ride a bicycle."

His eyebrows arched. "Are you making a point?"

"Yes. Age is only in the mind."

He smiled sardonically. "My mind is old, too."

"I'm sorry you couldn't have had children," she lied and felt guilty that she was glad about it. "Sometimes they make a marriage work."

"Sometimes they end it," he retorted.

"Fifty-fifty chance."

"Elise would never have risked her figure to have a child," he said coldly. "She even said so." He grimaced. "We had a hell of a fight after the Christmas I spent here. It disgusted me that she'd go to some party with her friends and not even bother to call to see how I was. She actually said to me the money was nice. It was a pity I came with it."

"I'm so sorry," she said with genuine sympathy. "I can't imagine the sort of woman who'd marry a man for what he had. I couldn't do that, even if I was dirt-poor."

He looked up into soft, pretty gray eyes. "No," he agreed. "You're the sort who'd get down in the mud with your husband and do anything you had to do to help him. Rare, Niki. Like that hothouse orchid pin I gave you for Christmas."

She smiled. "I wear it all the time. It's so beautiful."

"Like you."

She made a face. "I'm not beautiful."

"What's inside you is," he replied, and he wasn't kidding.

She flushed a little. "Thanks."

He drew in a breath and shuddered. "Oh, God…" He shot out of the bed, heading toward the bathroom. He barely made it to the toilet in time. He lost his breakfast and about a fifth of bourbon.

When he finished, his stomach hurt. And there was Niki, with a wet washcloth. She bathed his face, helped him to the sink to wash out his mouth then helped him back to bed.

He couldn't help remembering his mother, his sweet French mother, who'd sacrificed so much for him, who'd cared for him, loved him. It hurt him to remember her. He'd thought Elise resembled her. But it was this young woman, this angel, who was like her.

"Thanks," he managed to croak out.

"You'll be all right," she said. "But just in case, I'm going downstairs right now to hide all the liquor."

There was a lilt in her voice. He lifted the wet cloth he'd put over his eyes and peered up through a growing massive headache. She was smiling. It was like the sun coming out.

"Better hide it good," he teased.

She grinned. "Can I get you anything before I leave?"

"No, honey. I'll be fine."

Honey. Her whole body rippled as he said the word. She tried to hide her reaction to it, but she didn't have the experience for such subterfuge. He saw it and worried. He couldn't afford to let her get too attached to him. He was too old for her. Nothing would change that.

She got up, moving toward the door.

"Niki," he called softly.

She turned.

"Thanks," he said huskily.

She only smiled, before she went out and closed the door behind her.

Don't miss
WYOMING RUGGED by Diana Palmer,
available December 2015 wherever
Harlequin® HQN books and ebooks are sold.
www.Harlequin.com

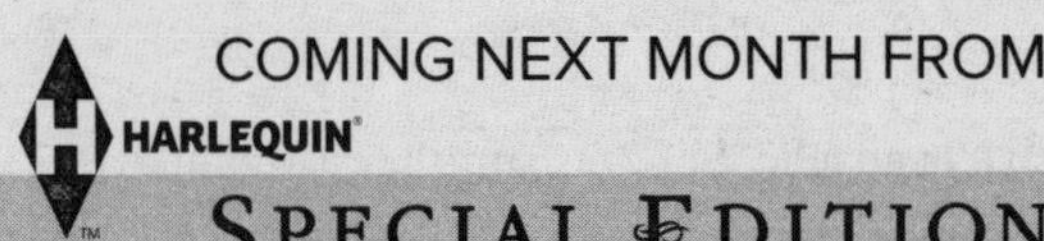

Available December 15, 2015

#2449 Fortune's Secret Heir
The Fortunes of Texas: All Fortune's Children
by Allison Leigh

The last thing Ella Thomas expects when she's hired to work a fancy party is to meet Prince Charming...yet that's what she finds in millionaire businessman Ben Robinson. But can the sexy tech mogul open up his heart to find his very own Cinderella?

#2450 Having the Cowboy's Baby
Brighton Valley Cowboys
by Judy Duarte

Country singer Carly Rayburn wants to focus on her promising singing career—so she reluctantly cuts off her affair with sexy cowboy Ian McAllister. But when she discovers she's pregnant with his child, she finds so much more in the arms of the rugged rancher.

#2451 The Widow's Bachelor Bargain
The Bachelors of Blackwater Lake
by Teresa Southwick

When real estate developer Sloan Holden meets beautiful widow Maggie Potter, he does his best to resist his attraction to the single mom. But a family might just be in store for this Blackwater Lake trio...one that only Sloan, Maggie and her daughter can build together!

#2452 Abby, Get Your Groom!
The Camdens of Colorado
by Victoria Pade

Dylan Camden hires Abby Crane to style his sister for her wedding...but his motives aren't pure. To make amends for the Camden clan's past wrongdoings, Dylan must make Abby aware of her past. But what's a bachelor to do when he falls for the very girl he's supposed to help?

#2453 Three Reasons to Wed
The Cedar River Cowboys
by Helen Lacey

Widower Grady Parker isn't looking to replace the wife he's loved and lost. Marissa Ellis is hardly looking for love herself—let alone with the handsome husband of her late best friend. But fate and Grady's three little girls have other ideas!

#2454 A Marine for His Mom
Sugar Falls, Idaho
by Christy Jeffries

When single mom Maxine Walker's young son launches a military pen pal project, she's just glad her child has a male role model in his life. But nobody expected Gunnery Sergeant Matthew Cooper to steal the hearts of everyone in the small town of Sugar Falls, Idaho—especially Maxine's!

When tycoon Ben Robinson enlists temp Ella Thomas to help him uncover Fortune family secrets, will the closed-off Prince Charming be able to resist the charms of his beautiful Cinderella?

Read on for a sneak preview of FORTUNE'S SECRET HEIR, the first installment in the 2016 Fortunes of Texas twentieth anniversary continuity, ***ALL FORTUNE'S CHILDREN****.*

Ben figured it was only a matter of time before the security guards came to check that he'd exited. But having gotten what he'd come for, he had no reason to stay.

He went out the door and it closed automatically behind him. When he tested it out of curiosity, it was locked.

"Crazy old bat," he muttered under his breath.

But he didn't really believe it.

Kate Fortune was many things. Of that he was certain.

But crazy wasn't one of them.

He looked around, getting his bearings before setting off to his left. It was dark, only a few lights situated here and there to show off some landscape feature. But he soon made his way around the side of the enormous house and to the front, which was not just well lit, but magnificently so. He stopped at the valet and handed over his ticket to a skinny kid in a black shirt and trousers.

He tried to imagine Ella dashing off the way this kid was to retrieve his car, parked somewhere on the vast property. He couldn't quite picture it.

HSEEXP1215

But in his head, he could picture *her* quite clearly.

Not the red hair. That just reminded him of Stephanie. But the faint gap in her toothy smile and the clear light shining from her pretty eyes.

That was all Ella.

A moment later, when the valet returned with his Porsche, Ben got in and drove away.

HSEEXP1215